COASTER'S MATE

by

WILFRID ROBERTSON

THE CHILDREN'S PRESS
LONDON AND GLASGOW

This edition 1968

PRINTED AND MADE IN GREAT BRITAIN

CONTENTS

CHAPTER ONE

FLYING ROOFS

THE tin-roofed seaport of Beira is never a cool spot at any time, and that evening the damp and muggy heat was exceptional, even for the coast of Portuguese East Africa in January.

Derek Ford, fresh out from England, felt as if all the vitality had been drained out of him. If he had had anything to do, or friends in the town, it would have been more bearable, but he had neither. In the rather doubtful hope that it might be cooler upstairs, he ascended to the broad upper veranda or balcony that circled the boarding-house where he was staying, and reached the bare-looking room that had been allotted to him.

Derek slipped off his clothes and threw himself on the bed, carefully retucking the mosquito-net that hung above it. He lay flat on his back, perspiring freely, and longing for the slightest puff of moving air. But none came through the wide-open doorway that gave access to the balcony, and the only sounds that broke the silence of the breathless night were occasional muffled footsteps passing along the sandy street below, the piping of mosquitoes outside the protective net, and the distant murmur of thunder far out at sea.

Time passed, and at length, despite the heat, Derek fell asleep.

Shortly after midnight Derek was awakened by a violent tugging and jerking at his bed. The stillness of the night was gone, and the wind was rushing in madly through the open doorway. The jerking that had roused him was the demented flapping and plucking of the mosquito-net above him.

Untucking a corner of the net he slipped out of bed to close the half-glass double doors against the gale. As Derek's bare feet touched the floor the wind was followed by rain, which lashed across the wide balcony and into the room in horizontal rods of water. A second later the mosquito-net tore itself clear of both bed and ceiling-fastening, shot across the room, and hung, a shapeless mass, against the opposite wall—pinned there by the force of the hurricane.

As the wind beat the sleep from his young body Derek began to realise what was happening. The excessive heat of the previous evening was explained. At that season of the year cyclones not uncommonly arise out of the wide stretch of sea between the East African coast and the distant island of Madagascar, and this time one of them had struck the town.

Against the incoming blast Derek struggled across the dark room and managed to close the half-glass doors. The wind and rain beat against them with a roar, making them quiver and tremble. With the shutting out of the wind the mosquito-net, deprived of its support, dropped limply to the floor.

A vivid flash of blue-white lightning lit up the interior of the room with a momentary blaze lighter than day, followed instantly by the ear-splitting crash of the thunder. As if this had been the signal, the straining doors burst their fastenings and slammed back violently on their hinges, sending the shattered glass from the upper panels flying like bomb-splinters. In swept the rain, almost a solid mass of water, striking clean against the opposite wall and soaking everything in its path.

Derek knew that the floor was littered with broken glass and before doing anything else he must get something on his bare feet. The next flash revealed his boots lying where he had placed them beside the bed; he secured them and then crossed over to where he remembered the electric light switch was situated.

He snapped it on, but there was no response—something had gone wrong with the current. Even had it been intact it would have been of little use to him, for a moment later the wildly swinging bulb and shade that hung from the ceiling snapped its wire and joined the general ruin on the floor.

Derek put in some quick thinking. Though he might manage to get the doors together again, and wedge them by dragging up the bed, the shattered panels would let in almost as much water. Moreover, every instant the hurricane was becoming more violent, causing the whole building to rock—would it not be better if he cleared out and got down to ground level before the whole upper part of it collapsed? What decided him was a rending crash, audible even above the roar of the elements, as the galvanised-iron roof of the balcony was torn from its fastenings and hurled away into the darkness.

Derek seized his day-clothes, tucked them under his arm, and made for the opening. He clung for a moment to the doorpost, and gained the balcony.

The force of the wind almost beat the breath from his body, and the lashing rain, warm as tea, poured off him in streams, ripping his thin pyjamas and nearly plucking the bundle from under his arm. With his hands against the wall he made his way along, feeling for the opening that led to the stairs and the ground floor.

Just as he reached it a human body almost collided with him and a hand gripped his arm. At that instant another brilliant flash tore across the sky, and by its light Derek recognised one of his fellow boarders, a tall dark man several years older than himself, and obviously English. As their eyes met in the momentary radiance the stranger grinned and shouted something but what he said was utterly lost in the uproar.

A couple more steps, and both were safely inside and at the head of the stairs. It was not until they had reached the ground level, however, where the surrounding walls partially muted the noise of the cyclone, that a human voice could be heard.

"I was coming to look for you," the stranger announced. "Noticed you about and guessed you were out from home."

"Frightfully good of you," Derek shouted back.

"Not at all. Whew! Listen to that!" he added, as a rending crash sounded from somewhere overhead, followed by the rumble and thump of bricks falling on the floor above. "Sounds as if the roof's gone, or part of it. Glad I'm not at sea to-night. But what about some light?"

The scrape of a match followed, and the man produced a candle from his pocket and put the flame to the wick. "I pinched this out of old Manoel's storeroom. As all the lights have fused I reckoned it might be useful."

"Where are the rest of them, the proprietor and the others?" Derek asked, for there were no signs of anyone else about.

The other jerked a thumb in the direction of the room where the meals were served, and grinned. "In yonder, and probably by now they've taken refuge under the table, each howling appeals to a different saint. Feel like joining 'em? No, I didn't think you would. I know a better spot—come along."

By the light of the candle Derek followed his new friend, and entered a small back room that he had not previously seen. " It's Manoel's private den," he was told, " but as he's elsewhere we might as well use it. Unless the whole place collapses it's as good here as anywhere."

The speaker stuck the candle upright in its own grease on the edge of the table and dropped into a chair. " That," he added, as another crash shook the trembling building, " is the remains of the roof, I should think. Half the town'll probably be roofless by morning, and most of the shipping in the Pungwe estuary piled up ashore."

" And a good many casualties too, I expect," Derek put in.

" Possibly, but I doubt it. Anybody with sense will have gone to ground when it started, as people do in an air-raid, though there may be some corpses among those flimsy erections in the native location beyond the Chiveve Creek. Anyway, there's nothing to be done at the moment except lie low and wait till it's over." He sat down in one of the chairs that the room contained. " Meanwhile we might as well make ourselves comfortable, and I'd advise you to scrap those remains of your pyjamas and put on the clothes you're carrying. They look a bit drier than what you have on, young fellow. What's your name, by the way? Mine's Carmichael."

Derek told him, adding that he had arrived only a few days previously.

" And landed yourself in difficulties right at the start," Carmichael remarked, indicating the uproar outside with a wave of his hand.

" I was in difficulties before that," Derek replied, as he changed into damp but slightly drier garments. " You see, I came out to take up a job which had been arranged through a London agent, but when I got here I found the concern had gone out of business, so I was stranded." He added the name of the firm.

"Those people? Yes, I'd heard they'd gone bust," Carmichael commented.

"I put up at a hotel for the first night or two," Derek went on, "but I soon realised it was much more than I could afford."

"So you shifted to this foul hole?" Carmichael put in. "Oh well, perhaps that's a bit strong—it's not so bad, and certainly it's cheap. My reasons for being here are much the same as yours. You wouldn't think, would you, that I'm not only master of a ship but an owner as well?"

Derek certainly would not. For one thing, though Carmichael was older than himself, he looked too young to be what he claimed. Ship-owners were usually elderly persons with well-filled waistcoats, not vigorous young men clad in worn shirts and trousers.

Carmichael read the disbelief in Derek's face and went on to explain. The coasting steamer, largely manned by a native crew, of which he had been both owner and skipper, had been sunk in a collision off the mouth of the river, and Carmichael had been forced to hang about in Beira waiting for the insurance claim to be settled. This, it appeared, had just been done. With the compensation he hoped to replace his lost vessel, and continue his voyages with cargo up and down the coast.

He was beginning to enlarge on the difficulties of finding a suitable ship for sale when his words were interrupted in a startling fashion. A mass of plaster crashed down upon the table, knocking over the candle, but Derek was able to grab and hold it upright again before the flame went out.

Both pairs of eyes glanced upwards. The remaining plaster of the ceiling was already grey with wet, and through the laths exposed by what had fallen, water was already beginning to pour.

" So I was right—it was the roof going that I heard," was Carmichael's remark. " The room above this must be open to the sky. I don't know what you think, but if somewhere drier than this exists, we'd better look for it."

Derek nodded, and the two emerged again at the foot of the staircase. The floor beneath their feet was already awash, and from the ejaculations that drifted to their ears from the direction of the dining-room where Manoel and his friends had taken refuge, it appeared that conditions there were not much better. But beneath the stairs there was a roomy cupboard that seemed comparatively dry, being well protected by the treads overhead, and the two took possession of it.

Ever since they had met both Derek and Carmichael had been forced to speak loudly to make themselves heard, but they had not been in their new refuge more than a few minutes when the all-pervading uproar ceased abruptly. Derek wondered for a moment if he had gone suddenly deaf, but Carmichael soon enlightened him.

" It's the centre of the cyclone passing over," he commented. " This calm will last for ten minutes, maybe, and then the wind'll slam down harder than ever from exactly the opposite quarter. Don't you think it's over yet—it won't be this side of dawn if I'm any judge. Let's take advantage of the lull to go and scrounge something to eat and drink out of Manoel's storeroom. Save it from being spoilt, and I don't fancy we'll see much in the way of breakfast in the morning."

They secured the rations and were back in the cupboard under the stairs in good time before the hurricane slammed down again. As Carmichael had prophesied, it did so with even greater fury than before, and every moment Derek expected that the walls of the building itself would crumble under the onslaught.

By the light of the guttering candle the two ate the food they had commandeered, and made themselves as comfortable as circumstances would allow. They sat without speaking, for there was no point in straining their voices.

Time passed, and at length there was a perceptible lessening of the din outside.

" I think that's the lot," Carmichael remarked, stretching his arms. " It's dying away into a drizzle, and by sunrise there'll probably be a clear sky and a gentle breeze. Any idea what time it is? "

Derek glanced at his wrist watch, thankful that he had not taken it off when he went to bed, or he might never have found it again in the turmoil of escaping from the room. " I make it a quarter past five."

" It begins to get light about half past," was the other's comment, " and then we'll be able to make a move and see what's what."

Presently the two emerged from their refuge, to find that the candle was no longer needed. The half-light of the dawn was filtering down from above the top of the stairs, and the sky was visible where the roof and part of a wall was missing. Every moment the light increased, for day comes rapidly in the tropics.

Others in the building were also astir. The proprietor passed them, waving his arms and bewailing the damage to his property. Derek and Carmichael meanwhile moved towards the door leading to the street, their feet crunching on the fallen plaster and rubbish that littered the sodden floor.

Though the bolts that had secured it at bedtime were still in their sockets, the door was half open, for it had been driven from its hinges by the impact of a flying sheet of corrugated iron. It took a few minutes to clear the aperture so that they could pass through, and then Derek and Carmichael emerged into the open.

The street presented a very different aspect compared with the previous evening. The rising sun revealed a scene of destruction. The ornamental trees that lined the sidewalks were battered and broken, and the road itself was littered with twisted sheets of corrugated iron and a tangle of wires from fallen telegraph-poles.

A glance at the buildings opposite showed that hardly one had failed to sustain damage. Several of them, like Manoel's boarding-house, had lost their entire roofs, while those which had not been decapitated as if by some vast axe presented a picture of collapsed verandas, broken windows, and slatted shutters hanging awry. The one redeeming feature was that the sandy ground on which the town was built had sucked away the torrential rain, so that flooding was not added to the other discomforts.

" Looks like plenty of work in prospect, putting all this straight," Carmichael remarked. " I expect the Portuguese authorities will have a general round-up for volunteers among their own crowd."

" We might give a hand too," said Derek. " I'm at a loose end—I don't know how you feel about it ? "

" Of course. Let's have a look at things first, and find out where we're likely to be needed most. I don't fancy being roped in on any old job."

CHAPTER TWO

THE SHIP ON THE SAND

DESPITE the early hour, Derek and Carmichael were not the only people about. On the East African coast it is the custom for shops and offices to open at dawn and close between ten and three during the heat of the day, and hurrying figures continually passed them, hastening to see what damage their places of business had sustained.

As the two made their way, stepping over the debris, towards the main thoroughfare of the town, the freakish tricks played by the previous night's tempest became apparent. Here four or five houses in a row would be unroofed, while next to them half a street would reveal no damage whatever. There a flimsy galvanised-iron erection stood firm, alongside a far more solid building that looked as if it had been bombarded.

Carmichael had been living in the town for some time, and knew several of the people whom he and Derek encountered. From them he gleaned the latest news of the situation.

From one it was learned that nobody apparently had been killed, though a number of persons, especially in the native location, had been cut or otherwise injured. Another explained the failure of the electric light right at the beginning of the cyclone, owing to the demolition of the local power-station; while a third remarked that all communications with the outside world were broken, cables and telegraph wires being smashed and the railway line up-country completely washed away.

" I think the best thing we can do," Carmichael said to Derek, " is to go over to the British-owned railway concession on the other side of the Chiveve Creek—you heard what one of those chaps said about the warehouses having ' caught a packet.' I know the local traffic manager fairly well, and I expect he'd be glad of help."

As they made their way in that direction they came in sight of the anchorage, and here another scene of devastation met their eyes. Ships that the evening before had been placidly moored in the estuary were no longer there; despite their double anchors most of them had dragged and were aground. Indeed some of the smaller vessels, together with a score of lighters, were perched high and dry on the sandy shore, or thrust deep among the mangroves.

Carmichael and Derek crossed the damaged bridge over the Chiveve Creek and passed through the gates of the Railway Concession. Here, oddly enough, they were on British territory, for the coastal terminus of the Rhodesia Railways is held on long lease from the Portuguese Government of Mozambique, and has its own regulations, police, and post office.

A glance showed that here there was plenty to do. Though the station offices themselves were almost intact, two of the big warehouses beyond them were crushed as if they had been stamped upon by a gigantic boot, and several overturned trucks lay on the adjacent sidings.

In contrast to the apathetic and bewildered attitude of the Portuguese town, the Railway Concession was humming with activity. Gangs of natives in the charge of the railway people were removing goods from the collapsed buildings and finding room for them elsewhere, clearing the rails, and righting the trucks with a portable crane. The arrival of Carmichael and Derek was heartily welcomed, directions were given and a gang allotted to them, and they were soon hard at work.

During the midday rest they returned to the boarding-house and removed their scanty belongings which were lying in their ruined rooms, for quarters had been offered them at the station which they were glad to accept.

It was on the second day of the new job that Carmichael heard of the *Chiwi*.

After a long day's work in the steamy atmosphere, he and Derek were eating their evening meal when one of the dock foremen from the railway wharf dropped in for a chat and a smoke. For a while they talked of this and that, and presently Carmichael spoke of the collision that had deprived him of both ship and job, of the recent settlement of the insurance claim, and of the difficulty in finding another suitable vessel.

" Why don't you have a try for the *Chiwi*? " was what the visitor asked.

" Let's see—oh, yes, I remember her. She was seized by the Portuguese a week or two ago, and her master and others clapped in jail. She'd be just about the tonnage I want—about a thousand or twelve hundred—but I'd no idea she was for sale."

" Aye, she is. She's to be auctioned come Thursday, I've heard tell. As maybe you know, she's aground on the Spit where the cyclone put her, but I doubt if she's damaged. Maybe she might go cheap—I ain't heard of anyone else wantin' her. Her late skipper and mate won't have no further interest in her for the next few years," he added with a grin. " Heaven save me from the inside of a prison on this coast! "

" What have they been up to? " asked Derek, scenting a yarn.

"Liquor smuggling," the visitor replied. "Somebody blundered, I suppose, or talked too freely, and they were caught by that Portuguese destroyer that does the coast patrol. Good job too."

"It's like this," Carmichael explained, knowing Derek was new to the country and ignorant of local affairs. "Natives can brew as much as they like of their own beer, which does them no harm whatever, but white men's spirits are a very different matter. Spirits make them lose all sense of control and turn them fighting mad, so there are stringent laws against them obtaining supplies. There is a certain class of native, however, probably those who have worked at some time in a town and got a taste of the stuff, who will pay almost anything for the crudest brands of gin and dop and arrak, and where there's a demand there's likely to be a supply."

"Yes, I suppose that would be so."

"Recently it's been an open secret that a lot of cheap rot-gut liquor has been circulating," Carmichael went on, "despite the efforts of the authorities and, I may add, those of the decent natives and village headmen, who see the harm it is doing."

"Ay, that's so," the dock foreman put in. "You wouldn't think it, but I've even heard some of my native stevedores, who you'd think 'ud be a tough lot, cursing the traffic in a way that 'ud delight a blue-ribbon temperance meeting at home! It's been a job to catch the blighters in the act, considering the hundreds of miles of lonely coast-line. But I guess that racket's settled now, good and proper."

"Perhaps, and perhaps not," Carmichael commented. "It doesn't follow that a business is stopped because one end of it is broken up. However, that's not our affair— what interests me is the vessel. I'd better have a look at her before Thursday. You say she's aground on the Spit?"

"Ay, you can walk all round her at low tide."

"As things are a bit easier now I might take a morning off to-morrow." Carmichael glanced at Derek. "Care to come with me?"

"Yes, I'd like to."

"Right. Then I'll see our boss in the morning and let him know we'll be off duty."

After an early breakfast Derek and Carmichael left the railway property and re-entered the town. They found the streets fairly clear of debris, and the sound of hammers and saws echoed through the morning air, for the towns-folk had by now recovered from their initial shock and were setting to work on necessary repairs.

As the two left the main street for a side-turn that would take them clear of the buildings and so to the dunes and sandy shore of the estuary, they heard a patter of bare feet behind them. Carmichael turned his head, and gave a grunt of recognition.

The man who had caught up with them was a half-bred Arab from Zanzibar, clad in a long garment that had once been white, and with a faded fez perched on his head. A broad grin split his brown face, exposing excellent teeth.

"Hallo, Yoruba, where have you come from?" said Carmichael. "I should have thought by now you'd have signed on with some other vessel." He spoke in a language that Derek did not then understand—it was Swahili, the language commonly used in East Africa by men of Yoruba's type.

"No, master, I have been waiting until you get another ship."

"Well, I'm in the way of doing so, I hope," was the reply, and Carmichael added a few details.

Yoruba nodded. With the faculty these men have for absorbing information, he seemed to know all about the *Chiwi* and the coming auction. " That ship is the kind we need," he added, speaking as if he were a partner in the business. " If Allah wills we will buy and sail in her. You go to look at her? I will come too."

Yoruba dropped into step behind them, and as they continued their way, Carmichael explained to Derek who the man was.

" He was my ' capitao '—the head-boy of my crew, you know—in my vessel which was sunk. First-class fellow, and the best pilot I've struck, for he knows every inch of the coast. I relied on him a lot, especially as I and another chap I had with me were the only white men aboard. If I get this vessel, I wonder how many of my old crew I can get hold of."

" Fellows like this chap? " Derek asked.

" All kinds, and every colour from mid-brown to jet-black, and good, bad, and indifferent. One I'd like to get again is my old engineer—he's a Cape-boy with an astounding flair for engines of the type they have in these coasters, though a bit of a rogue in some ways." Carmichael glanced over his shoulder. " Seen anything of Half-crown lately, Yoruba? "

" Yes, master, like me he waits till we buy our new ship."

" Oh, he does, does he? Where's he now? "

" Yonder, where we are going."

" The deuce he is! And what's he doing there? "

Yoruba looked embarrassed, and Carmichael gave a short laugh. " What's the betting," he remarked to Derek, " that Half-crown's heard of the coming auction, and has gone to scrounge what he can beforehand. He'll pinch anything that isn't nailed down, though I'll admit

he was honest enough over my things when he was working for me. He'll get a surprise when we appear."

Derek laughed. " Lives up to his name, and fond of
money, eh? But why ' Half-crown '—I thought ' Six-
pence ' was the popular name for these southern boys? "

Carmichael snorted. " I fancy he did call himself that
once, but since the cost of living's gone up, he felt it didn't
conform with his dignity! "

At last they came in sight of the vessel they sought.
Her bow rested well above the tidemark, while a foot of
water lapped round her stern, which, at dead low tide,
would also be high and dry. She was of the common type
of coasting steamer, with rust-streaked sides painted
black, and a single straight funnel rising abaft the small
bridge and wheel-house. She lay upon the sand on an
even keel and with hardly any list, and except that both
her boats were missing from the davits she did not appear
outwardly to have suffered any great damage from the
cyclone.

A broken anchor-chain hung down from her bow, and
by its aid Derek and Carmichael scrambled aboard. With
Yoruba following they moved aft.

As they rounded a corner of the main deck-house a
figure, clad in a greasy shirt and trousers, nearly collided
with them. The man pulled up with a startled exclamation, first alarm, and then tardy recognition, written on
his dusky face.

" So you're aboard after all? " Carmichael remarked
sourly. " Seems to me you've been making the most of
your time."

There was certainly good cause for the comment.
Half-crown's arms were full of a miscellaneous collection
of fittings, ranging from the ship's chronometer, un-
screwed from the chart-room wall, to the brass taps

belonging to the wash-basin in the master's cabin. However, he pulled himself together, gave a deprecating grin, and pleaded justification.

" 'Mornin', baas. Sell these for a lot o' money. Why leave for Portuguese police to pinch before they sell ship to new owner?"

" As it happens, I hope to be the new owner."

" Oh, that very different, baas. If they going to be ours "—again that possessive pronoun—" I put 'um back where I took 'um."

" You'd better, and get a move on with it. And when you've done it come down to the engine-room, and if I'm not there, wait for me. If I buy the vessel I'm going to make sure you understand her engines before I sign you on again. Otherwise I'll get someone else."

Half-crown's only reply was an expressive click of disgust at the mere suggestion that he could not handle efficiently any marine engine ever constructed. Picking up his loot he vanished from sight to set about his task of restitution.

Carmichael was aware that the *Chiwi* was to be disposed of just as she lay, without any guarantee, the onus being on the buyer to get her afloat again. But before going into that problem he meant to satisfy himself that the vessel was reasonably sound. From deck to bridge and from engine-room to the empty holds he moved, pausing at times to ask Yoruba a question or listen to some comment that issued from Half-crown's thick lips. He did not hurry over the inspection, and most of the morning was gone before he had finished.

" Well, what do you think of her?" Derek asked when they finally emerged on deck.

" She's quite sound as far as I can see and, though at the moment it's impossible to be certain, I don't think she's holed anywhere. She's stoutly built, there are no rocks here, and she's resting on sand. Let's drop overside and have a look at what sort of a problem getting her off is going to be."

By way of the broken anchor-chain they regained the sand, passing round her hull and pausing for a moment to make sure that the propeller-blade had not been bent out of the true. By this time the tide had fully ebbed, and it was possible to walk right round her. As they reached the strip of wet sand separating the beached vessel from the opaque and muddy waters of the Pungwe estuary, an unexpected snag was revealed.

The falling tide had exposed a low, whale-backed ridge of sand lying between the *Chiwi* and deep water. The violence of the cyclone had clearly lifted the vessel right over it and deposited her on the landward side.

"That's a bit of a jolt," said Carmichael. He pulled a pipe from his pocket, filled and lighted it, frowning at the long hummock meanwhile. "At the top of high water it might be possible to kedge her off a sloping beach, but you can't pull a thousand tons uphill."

"Wouldn't it be possible to dig it away sufficiently at slack water when the tide is out?" Derek suggested.

"Oh, yes, but it would take some time, a good gang of natives, and quite a lot spent out in wages. However, there'd be no alternative. At least I know how I stand before I attend that auction on Thursday. Well, I've seen all I want—let's be getting back."

They turned their faces towards the town. As they walked Derek made one or two remarks, but received only grunts for replies. Carmichael seemed deep in thought, and they completed their journey in unbroken silence.

CHAPTER THREE

AN OFFER AND A WARNING

THURSDAY came, and Carmichael went to attend the auction of the *Chiwi*.

Derek watched him go, and turned to resume what he was doing. But for once his heart was not in his work, for he was feeling worried and depressed.

Repairs of the damage caused by the cyclone were nearly completed, and in a day or two he realised he would once more be at a loose end. The scanty store of money with which he had arrived was dwindling, and there seemed no prospect of finding a suitable job. Neither the railways nor those British firms who had branches in the town wanted anybody, and the language question alone precluded any chance with a Portuguese concern.

Seeking elsewhere was at present impossible, for the railway line up-country to Rhodesia was still out of action. Nor could he even cable home for money. The only means of communication between the isolated town and the outside world was by the wireless of one of the liners in the port to some passing ship far out at sea, which would transmit to the first land station with which contact was made. But this method was confined almost entirely to government and official messages.

The prospect of the immediate future, therefore, was not bright. Unless he could secure a billet within the next few days, Derek realised he would find himself in an unpleasant situation, and he shrank from the idea of being forced to apply to the British consul for the meagre dole issues to a " Distressed British Subject."

The prospect of Carmichael's probable departure added to Derek's depression. Though they had only met a few days before they had become good friends, and he would miss that companionship considerably.

Listlessly he continued his work, and at length came the time to knock off. Derek dismissed the gang of natives with a gesture, and returned to the temporary quarters which he and Carmichael were occupying.

Carmichael was already back from the sale, and he greeted Derek with a cheerful nod. " Well, for better or worse it's done—I've bought her."

Derek pulled himself together, feeling he must shake off his own worries and take an interest.

" Were there many bidders? I hope you were able to get it at a reasonable price."

" I did. In fact, as the expression has it, I got her for a song, though I didn't think I should when I arrived. There were several men there, Portuguese from the town, and I expected competition. But not a bit of it— apparently they'd come out of curiosity and hardly one of them opened his mouth. There was a tentative bid at the start, probably arranged for by the auctioneer, and when I put in mine there was no higher offer."

" I suppose the problem of getting her afloat again choked them off," Derek commented.

" Maybe. Anyway their reasons don't matter a rap to me. I got her cheap, which gives me a useful balance in hand to spend on salvage and fitting. A fresh batch of ship's papers are being made out, which I'm to call for at the Port Office on Monday. Meanwhile I must get in touch with Yoruba and Half-crown again, and tell them that the *Chiwi* is now mine."

Carmichael went on to speak of his plans—how Yoruba must round up any of his old crew that might still be available and recruit others to make up the required number, and also what his intentions were in the matter of the obstructing sandbank and getting the *Chiwi* water-borne once more. Derek listened, putting in a comment when circumstances seemed to call for one, but half the time he found his attention wandering, for his mind was still full of the problem of his own immediate future.

Presently he realised that Carmichael was passing on to another point.

"The fellow I had with me as mate went south after that collision," he was saying. "I shall have to get some-one else. Must have two white men aboard so that there's always one in charge. The difficulty is to find the right man—and always remembering one's got to live at close quarters with him." Laughing, Carmichael glanced at Derek, and noticed the preoccupied look on his face.

"Wake up! I don't believe you're listening."

"Yes, I am," Derek replied, jerking his mind back to the present. "A bit tired, perhaps, after the day's work, but I've heard all you've been telling me."

"Well, I've got something to suggest. You're out of a job, and candidly I don't see you getting one hereabouts, so what about shipping with me? We know each other and you're not afraid of work. What about it?"

Derek sat upright, his former listlessness gone.

"It's jolly decent of you, and there's nothing I should like better. Though I came out here with an office job in view, I wasn't keen about it. But——" He paused.

"But what?"

"I know nothing whatever about seamanship. I'd be

useless to you. You'd much better sign on someone who——"

"Cut that out," Carmichael interrupted. "You'll pick up what's needed as we go along. Though you may be nominally mate, what I really want is someone to be around when I'm having a watch below."

"Then I'll accept gladly, and do my best to get the hang of things quickly. But there's one other point: aren't there regulations about a mate's qualifications before he's allowed to sign on?"

Carmichael grinned. "Not in this part of the world. There's no fatherly British Board of Trade to come nosing round and asking questions. Nobody worries much about what goes on aboard a coasting tramp. Coming?"

"Rather!"

"That's good." Carmichael held out his hand to seal the compact. "We'll buy some stores for present use, shift over to the *Chiwi* to-morrow, and get down to the job before us."

By the following noon Carmichael and Derek had fixed up their quarters aboard. Yoruba, who had once more appeared just when he was wanted, had been dispatched to round up any of his old companions who were available, while Half-crown was down in the engine-room preparing for the day when the vessel should be afloat again.

It was not until sunset that Yoruba returned, bringing with him three of Carmichael's former crew, the only ones that had not been taken on elsewhere. To Derek this seemed disappointing but Carmichael was confident that they would soon get the full number required; for the news that hands were wanted would filter round the native quarter and the eating-houses that such men frequent.

He was right. On the following morning quite a little crowd were waiting on the sand, some wanting to be taken on as deck-hands and others as stokers. Carmichael questioned them and made a selection of the likeliest looking applicants, and having made up the number required dismissed the rest. Those chosen came aboard, and were sent to the crew's quarters to deposit the bundles of personal baggage they carried.

It was not long afterwards that Half-crown emerged from the engine-room and went forward. Derek heard the sound of angry voices, and presently the man came out again, a grievance written on his face. Carmichael was down on the sand with Yoruba, so he came straight to where Derek stood.

"One of these new men has pinched my bunk and thrown my blankets on the floor," he protested indignantly. "I come here first, I boss-boy, that bunk mine! You come, baas, and tell 'um that!"

Derek saw that it was a matter needing prompt settlement lest it should lead to a fight, and certainly Half-crown had the prior right. Though there might be language difficulties, Derek felt he could make himself understood, for the Cape-boy could translate what he said. He crossed over to the crew's quarters, from which a babel of chatter was now issuing.

"Stop that row!" Derek ordered sharply. "Now then, Half-crown, which is the fellow in question? This one? Well, tell him from me to put his blankets elsewhere."

Half-crown did so, adding forceful expressions of his own. His rival promptly turned to Derek, lodging a protest.

"What's he say?" Derek asked.

"He say that his bunk last voyage and voyage before," Half-crown translated. "These others," he added, indicating some of the bystanders, " have took their old bunks and he wants his."

Derek was startled. Was Carmichael aware that he had taken on several ex-members of the liquor smugglers' crew? He succeeded, however, in not showing his surprise in his face, and after giving orders to the new man to shift his things and find accommodation elsewhere, he left the fo'c'sle and went to report to his employer what he had learned.

Carmichael received the information with a shrug. " I rather suspected as much," he commented. " Surprised that the Portuguese haven't clapped them in prison along with the white men concerned? I'm not. Though probably these fellows knew what was going on, they'd have no option either way and have to obey orders, so the police have just told them to clear out and find other jobs. Anyway, as long as they prove to be good workers that's all that I care about."

Carmichael found no complaint on that score. Those among the new men who had once belonged to the *Chiwi's* crew turned out to be cheerful and willing, and quite a rivalry sprang up between them and the others as to who could shift the largest portion of the obstructing sandbank before the rising tide each day forced the work to cease.

At the end of a week of heavy labour with shovels, a cutting of sufficient depth had been dug through the sandbank, and preparations were made for the final act. An extra high tide was due in a few days, which, lapping round the grounded vessel, would make her partially buoyant, and with a kedge-anchor and cable attached to her cargo-windlass Carmichael hoped at the right moment to be able to haul the *Chiwi* off the sand.

The necessary wire and anchor had not appeared, and

Derek offered to go over to the town, interview the man who had agreed to lend them, and hasten delivery.

It took him some time to find the man he sought, but at length he made contact with him down at the railway wharf and secured his promise to have the required articles delivered on the following day. By the time the business was settled night had fallen, but the moon was near its full, and by its light Derek started on his return journey.

He left the main street for the side road with its bordering lines of shoddy dwellings and eating-houses frequented by the rougher elements of the town. From the open door of one of these latter places a broad beam of light streamed out, together with a babel of voices apparently engaged in a heated argument. As Derek neared the eating-house the figure of a man was violently propelled out of the door. He staggered away for a few yards, and finally collapsed in the roadway.

Derek's first thought was to pass on, for nightly rows were not uncommon and it was none of his business. After walking on a short distance he glanced back, and saw that the man still lay where he had fallen. Derek hesitated, wondering if the man were badly hurt. Reluctantly he decided that he had better return and see.

By the time he reached the spot the prostrate figure was beginning to stir. "Hallo, are you all right?" Derek asked, peering at the fellow in the moonlight.

He expected an answer in Portuguese, but the reply came in English, coupled with a strong smell of shag tobacco and cheap spirits.

"Aw, I'm okay. Gimme a hand up, mate."

With Derek's help the man got unsteadily to his feet, and with the back of a dirty hand wiped the blood that was trickling from a cut on his forehead. "Thank'ee, mate, you're a gennleman. Not like them blokes in there." He indicated the building from which he had been ejected. " We was havin' a nargument, y'understand, jus' a friendly yargument, but some coves can't 'old their tempers nohow."

" Plenty of chaps like that," Derek admitted, for something to say. " Feeling better now? Well, I'll be getting along. G'night."

" 'Ere arf a mo', mister." The man peered at Derek in the moonlight. " I've seen you afore—you're a-workin' for the bloke wot's bought the *Chiwi*, him that reckons to get her afloat and off to sea again."

" That's right," Derek replied.

The other gripped his arm and leaned forward, his evil-smelling breath wafting into Derek's face.

" You watch out, mister," he said in a hoarse whisper. " 'E got it cheap, didn't 'e? And for why? 'Cos them others was shy o' bidding, see? What about them blokes wot the Portugooses pinched 'er orf, eh? "

" They're **in** prison and likely to stop there," Derek replied, managing to release his arm and step back into a clearer atmosphere.

" Oh-ah, maybe, but there's others they ent cotched. I don't know nothin', mind you, or I'd tell you, I would, for you've acted like a gennleman 'elpin' me up off of the street, and I'd do anythin' to 'elp a pal, I would. So you take my tip, mister, and watch out, I says," and having unburdened himself he slowly sank into a sitting position in the middle of the sandy road, where he felt more secure than on his shaky legs.

With a shrug Derek continued his journey, ruminating over the fellow's words and wondering whether he ought to mention the encounter to Carmichael. But as he walked on he decided that the tipsy mumblings of some

longshore loafer were not worth bothering about, and
by the time he reached his destination he had almost
forgotten the incident.

On the following morning, as promised, the heavy
kedge-anchor and wire cable arrived in a creaking ox-cart
and were unloaded on to the sand. At dead low tide the
kedge was carried out as far as possible and sunk into the
bed of the estuary, while the wire was brought back over
the *Chiwi's* stern to the drum of her after winch.

The winch was small and of no great power, and
Derek felt doubtful of its efficacy towards getting the
vessel off, but as Carmichael pointed out, there would be
other helping factors. The high tide would give partial
buoyancy, and there was sufficient coal still lying in the
vessel's bunker to provide steam for both windlass and
main engine. With the propeller revolving astern and
the winch tugging at the cable, he contended there was
a good chance of success.

At length the time approached when the plan was to
be tested. Thoroughly in his element down below, Half-
crown watched the gauges and harried his firemen with
picturesque abuse as steam was raised in the boilers. The
rising tide crawled up over the sand and encircled the
vessel, and inch by inch it crept up her plates.

At last the long-awaited moment arrived. Carmichael
rang down to Half-crown for full speed astern, at the
same time lifting a hand to Yoruba, standing ready at
the winch lever, to get busy. The drum began to revolve
with a chuff and a clatter, bringing the wire up taut and
quivering, while beneath the *Chiwi's* counter the half-
submerged propeller thrashed up fountains of muddy
water.

A minute passed and then another, while the cable
vibrated and the blades sent foam swirling forward from

under the stern. And then, as Derek was beginning to feel that the effort was doomed to failure, there was a slight tremor beneath his feet.

" She's moving! " he shouted.

Carmichael, from where he stood, gave an answering wave. " Didn't I say so? " he retorted with a triumphant bellow.

Another tremor, much more pronounced than before, and the winch clattered as Yoruba was able to take up a couple of yards on the drum. The movement quickened, already her stern was waterborne. Then the bow slid clear, and the vessel was free of her sandy bed.

There could be no respite for rejoicing, however, for though the *Chiwi* was waterborne she was not yet clear of the cutting made through the now-submerged sandbank, and without prompt action the current of the river might swing and ground her against one side of the gap. Yoruba's winch clattered frantically as he wound in the slack of the sagging wire to prevent it from fouling the propeller, while Carmichael, his hands on the steering wheel and his head over his shoulder, swung her rudder to counteract the pull.

There was another minute of anxiety as the vessel moved onwards, stern first, towards deep water. At last, with a grunt of thankfulness, Carmichael thrust over the handle of the ship's telegraph to " stop."

While the kedge wire was being buoyed and cast off, to be collected later at low tide, he and Derek hastened below. Now that the vessel was off the sand and afloat, it could be discovered for certain whether she were holed anywhere along her bottom. One by one the bilges were tested, but, except for the sump that is usually found in vessels of this kind, they were dry, and there were no signs of the *Chiwi* making water anywhere.

CHAPTER FOUR

CARGO FOR ZANZIBAR

SECURED by a new anchor and chain which replaced the broken links hanging from her bow, the *Chiwi* lay moored not far from the railway wharf. Derek was standing on her deck, watching the approach of a rowing-boat that had pulled out from the concrete steps near the town.

The boat came alongside and Carmichael clambered aboard. " Any luck? " Derek asked as he stepped on to the deck.

" Very much so. I've fixed up for a full cargo, all for one consignee, which always pays better than a number of small lots to be delivered at potty little places along the coast. We've quite a long run before us, as far up as Zanzibar, where I hope we'll pick up return loads for dropping at ports on our way back."

" That's good. When do we start loading? "

" Within an hour I hope. The port tug'll be over soon to put us alongside the wharf. My goodness, I shan't be sorry to get away to sea again," Carmichael added with a heart-felt sigh, " I'm about fed up to the back teeth with Beira and everything to do with it! "

The next few hours was a time of noise and dirt. As soon as she was tied up, the *Chiwi* was invaded by a chattering horde of native stevedores, who tore off her hatch-covers and packed her holds, keeping pace with the swinging arm of the dock-side crane. An even dirtier and noisier period followed, as coal was shot into her bunker.

But at last the hatch-covers were once more in place and the wedges knocked home, the final stores and sundries came aboard, and the crew of the *Chiwi* made ready for sea.

It was with satisfaction that Carmichael and Derek watched the final act, the arrival on board of the Portuguese pilot who was to take the vessel down-river. Yoruba, however, though he should have looked cheerful considering that the vessel was bound for his home town of Zanzibar, eyed that unshaven individual with ill-concealed hatred. He loathed all pilots, feeling them to be a slur on his intimate knowledge of the coast, and he was only happy when putting in and out of tiny ports where such interfering creatures as official pilots did not exist.

On an ebbing tide the *Chiwi* passed down the estuary, its waters turgid and muddy from the silt brought down by the heavy rains up-country. At the mouth the engines were stopped for a minute so that Yoruba's detested rival could drop into the waiting launch. Carmichael then rang down to Half-crown for full speed, and the vessel began gently to rise and fall as she breasted the swell of the open sea.

Derek was amazed to find how quickly he was settling down to his new surroundings—already it seemed months since he had accepted Carmichael's offer and taken up his quarters aboard the beached coaster. Every part of her was now familiar ground to him, and her crew were now no longer just natives, but individuals with distinguishing characters and names. Under Carmichael's teaching he was rapidly gaining useful knowledge about his job, and lastly, with the help of a number of key words, he was picking up by ear something of the local dialects of the native hands.

That evening Derek experienced his first spell of duty

at sea, thus giving Carmichael a much-needed rest and sleep after all the bustle and anxiety of loading and departure. " Don't hesitate to call me if there's need," Carmichael had said, " though I don't expect you'll run up against any difficulty. The glass is steady and there should be no change in the weather, and Yoruba's doing duty at the wheel and he knows the course like the back of his hand."

Derek ascended to the *Chiwi's* bridge, where Yoruba stood at the wheel, steering in the drowsy fashion typical of the Arab half of his ancestry, whose dhows have sailed the East Coast in quest of slaves and gold and ivory since the days of Mahomet. His profile was outlined against the night by the faint glow of the binnacle, and Derek wondered if he ever troubled to check his bearing by compass. Though presumably he had been taught to read it, no doubt he relied far more on habit and the stars for holding a steady course.

Having made sure that the sidelights were burning properly, and that the look-out man on the fo'c'sle head was not asleep, Derek leaned his elbows on the rail and contemplated the serenity of the night.

The *Chiwi* was making a steady five or six knots, running parallel to the coast a few miles away to port, though the low shore was quite invisible. All around lay the wide expanse of water, unbroken by the steaming-lights of any other vessel, for big ships and liners lay their course much farther out to sea. Overhead the stars shone down from a clear sky, but low down to the west was a massive cloud-bank in and out of which the light-ning flickered continually, telling of heavy rain falling over the African bush and forest, for the wet season was still at its height.

Despite the slight breeze made by the motion of the

vessel, the air was hot and clammy. Though clad only in the singlet and trousers that are the " uniform " of the coasting trade, Derek felt his garments sticking to his skin, and heartily he pitied those whom big-ship discipline compelled to wear brass-bound jackets and collars and ties in the tropics.

Steadily the *Chiwi* snored her way onwards, the only sounds audible being the swish of the water as her bow clove the quiet sea, and the occasional clang of a shovel dropped by one of Half-crown's gang below. The track of the vessel's short foremast wrote its signature endlessly against the indigo vault above, and the smoke from her funnel rolled lazily astern in a trail like black cotton-wool. With nothing visible but sea and sky, Derek felt a strange peace enter his soul, as if he were alone with the Infinite. The world of men and money and worries seemed ten thousand miles away, and what might be happening there he neither knew nor cared. Nor could any word of it intrude even through the ether; for small coasters like the *Chiwi* are not fitted with wireless.

The vessel steamed northwards, and with each passing day Derek's knowledge of sea and ship and crew increased. Occasionally passing steamers were sighted, and as they drew nearer their destination, Arab dhows were not infrequent, sailing from the island of Zanzibar to obscure native ports along the coast.

One of them, lying close to the *Chiwi's* course, hailed her, waving cloths to attract attention and holding up some red earthenware pots. As their gestures seemed to indicate urgency, Carmichael stopped his engines and signalled to the motley crew to come alongside.

The dhow drew nearer, her pole mast and lateen sail suspended from a long curving spar swaying to the roll of the sea. Her skipper, an elderly and bearded Arab who in his youth had no doubt run many a cargo of slaves, was perched above her elaborately carved stern, his arms clasping the heavy teak beam of her tiller, while forward the three others who formed her crew were preparing to cast a native-made rope. Derek, watching from the *Chiwi's* rail, felt he was being given a glimpse of the misty past, for the East Coast dhow has not changed materially in pattern for two thousand years.

It was drinking-water they wanted—owing to adverse winds their voyage had taken longer than expected and every drop had been consumed. Carmichael was able to supply them with enough to fill their pots, and the old and the new in ship design parted company amid grins and chaff and the blessings of Allah.

At last the *Chiwi's* destination, the island of Zanzibar which lies some twenty miles off the coast, rose out of the sea. With every turn of the propeller its outline became more distinct, a place of undulating hills and white beaches fringed by groves of coconut palms. The town was hidden, being on the north-west side, but presently it came in sight, a clustering mass of white buildings, with the blue water of the anchorage in the foreground dotted with vessels ranging from liners to dhows.

The *Chiwi* steamed onwards, past a couple of tiny islets, and at length found her berth amongst the anchored shipping.

" There's no drawing up to the wharf here," Carmichael remarked to Derek. " Lighters will come alongside and we discharge into them. That means getting the derricks rigged and wire rove through the blocks and to the cargo-winches. Will you see to that? "

" If I can," Derek replied, conscious of his inexperience.

" Yoruba'll do the actual job, and probably Half-crown

will lend a hand when he's finished below, for only a small head of steam'll be needed for the winches. Your job'll be to keep 'em moving: I've got to go ashore and see our consignee, likewise call on one or two people I know, about getting fresh cargoes. I'll be back before long."

Carmichael turned to signal to one of the native craft that were already hovering expectantly round the *Chiwi*, and a minute later he was being rowed towards the landing-steps by a coal-black boatman clad in a tattered shirt and the remains of a crownless straw hat.

An hour later the lighters arrived alongside, together with a portly Indian who announced himself as the consignee's agent. Carmichael had not yet returned, and Derek was not quite sure what he ought to do. However, remembering the old adage—"Do *something*, even if it's wrong"—after a hasty consultation with Yoruba and Half-crown, he got the hatch-covers off and ordered discharging to begin.

At length, when Carmichael reappeared, he expressed approval. "That's right," he said, "the sooner we get the holds emptied the better. I've been some time, I know, but I've not wasted it. I've fixed up for three or four different consignments for various small places we passed on our way north." He glanced at the bustle going on round the after hatch. "They can get on with it by themselves for the present," he added. "Come down to the cuddy and we'll go through these particulars." He indicated a sheaf of papers that he carried.

Details of three of the prospective consignments were clear—two to small coast ports and a third for Beira. But the fourth puzzled him. "I know of a tiny place called Mandira and another called Mabina, but I've never heard of Malira. I wish I'd checked up before I left the town. Perhaps one of our crew may have heard of this place—I haven't."

He went out to inquire, but without result. "It must be one of those two, and I must find out which. Look here, I shall have to stop aboard, but what about you going ashore and seeing this fellow? Yoruba knows where he lives and can go with you as guide."

Derek agreed gladly, and it was not long before he was sitting in a leaky native boat on his way to the landing-steps.

Yoruba knew every inch of the town in which he had been born, and he led Derek by the most direct route to his destination, plunging into the tortuous lanes and alleys of the "bazaar."

To Derek it seemed as if he had stepped into another world, one that was wholly Eastern and having no relationship to the African continent only a few sea miles away.

Above him rose many-storeyed buildings, their upper windows screened by carved shutters, and their height creating a twilight gloom below. On either side of the narrow alleys were the open-fronted stalls of the grain-sellers, sweetmeat vendors, brass-workers, and dealers in pottery, silks, and inlay, while the air was stagnant with many pungent scents, those of cloves and copra—the two main products of the island—predominating.

Up and down the narrow lanes swarmed one of the most mixed crowds in the world; Arabs, Indians, and natives of East Africa—Moslems, Hindus, Parsees, and savage spirit-worshippers. Here Derek caught sight of a rich Parsee merchant, his ample paunch parting the crowd as the bows of a ship cleave the water; there he set eyes upon a bearded Arab, tall, high-nosed and aloof, as befitted one of the dominant race; here a well-to-do citizen, his white robe resplendent with scarlet and gold embroidery; there the skinny and half-naked figure of a water-carrier, his shoulders bowed under the weight of his filled goat-skin. Black "Zanzibaris," descendants of former slaves, jostled past with laden donkeys in tow, and occasionally Derek saw the veiled figure of a woman, with nothing visible of her face except a glimpse of dark eyes in the slit between her head-covering and yashmak.

At length Derek reached his desination, a house in the European quarter, and explained his errand. The error, it appeared, had been the fault of a half-caste typist, and the matter was soon made clear. Mabina was the place to which the consignment was destined, a tiny spot of trading-stores and shanties a couple of miles up a certain tidal river. Having got his information and chatted for a few minutes with Carmichael's friend, Derek retraced his steps towards the landing-stage.

Derek's appearance at the top of the steps was the signal for half a dozen boats to converge with much shouting and splashing of oars, each owner hoping to secure his custom. Yoruba selected the one he fancied, driving off the others with abuse couched in fluent Swahili, and held the gunwale steady against the concrete for his white companion to step aboard.

As Derek was about to do so he heard the patter of bare feet behind him, and he turned to see a black Zanzibari, draped in a long white garment, and bearing a letter in his hand. "You belong that steamah *Chiwi*?" he panted in English.

"Yes. Why?"

The fellow's only answer was to hold out the note he carried. Derek felt that there was probably some mistake, but he took the proffered missive and turned it over to read the name presumably written on the envelope.

There was none, however. It was merely addressed:

To the Master of *S.S. Chiwi.*

"Who gave you this? Where do you come from?" Derek demanded, looking up. But already the messenger was gone, slipping silently away among the loafers at the top of the steps.

"Odd," Derek muttered. "Know anything about him, Yoruba, or who sent him?"

Yoruba shook his head.

"No matter," thought Derek to himself as he stepped into the boat. "Obviously it's for Carmichael, and I suppose he'll know all about it."

When Carmichael opened the letter, however, he was as perplexed as Derek had been. Between a brief address at the top and the initials "C.M." at the bottom appeared only five words—"Come up and see me."

"Haven't a ghost of an idea who it's from—certainly nobody I know," Carmichael commented. "Somebody, too, who's pretty sparing with words." He considered for a minute, turning the note in his hand. "I feel inclined to ignore it, and yet—— It might be from someone who wants to ship cargo, though why he should send such a curt message I can't imagine. I suppose I'd better go and see him, whoever he may be."

CHAPTER FIVE

MILVERTON

FACING the main street, and not far from the chief hotel in Zanzibar, stood a tall building with a magnificently carved doorway, and lower windows heavily barred with ancient ironwork. It had once been the dwelling of a rich Arab trader, but its interior had now been divided into offices and flats, occupied by various tenants.

On the morning of the *Chiwi's* arrival at the anchorage one of these was sitting at a desk, deep in thought. He was a heavily built man with a florid face and wearing horn-rimmed spectacles. Though he held a pen in his hand, its nib had not touched paper for the last half hour. He was puzzling over a matter that had occupied his thoughts for the last three weeks. His name was Claude Milverton, and officially he described himself as an " agent "—a usefully elastic term that served to screen a good deal from the public eye.

The cause of his worry had been the receipt of a cablegram, brief and unsigned, but he guessed who had sent it.

" Consignment reached wrong address. Impossible contact forwarding agents at present. Await your further instructions," it had read.

To the transmitting telegraph officials it had seemed a normal commercial message, but to Milverton, knowing the code underlying the simple words, it had come as a nasty shock.

He had taken a day or two to consider, and then had carefully drafted an equally innocent-looking reply. To ensure that there should be no mistake, instead of sending his Zanzibari servant he had gone to dispatch it himself. But at the post office he had received another jar: owing to some unexplained reason, he was told, the cable to Beira had gone dead the evening before, and it was not possible to transmit any messages.

The cause of the interruption had been the cyclone, though it had been several days before that fact was known. On further inquiry at the post office, Milverton had been told that weeks might elapse before normal communications were restored, and that a letter mailed by the next south-bound steamer would probably get to Beira before that.

Having no alternative, Milverton wrote a guarded letter, but the knowledge that a long time must elapse before it could be received added to his mental discomfort. He longed for details, and cursed the sender of the cable for being so laconic.

Apparently the last consignment of smuggled liquor had been seized by the Portuguese authorities. But what of the vessel that had carried it? Had the *Chiwi* also been captured, or had she got away? The wording of the second sentence might imply that the skipper and mates (" forwarding agents ") could not be contacted because they had run her into some obscure creek and were lying low, or it might mean that the ship had been impounded and those in charge of her effectually locked up in prison.

In the latter case Milverton would be in a quandary. Another cargo awaited shipment at a Madagascar port, and without the *Chiwi* his means of running it over to the coast was gone. Yet it must be moved, and quickly, for the Madagascar dock people would not allow the stuff to remain and clutter up their wharfage indefinitely. Already Milverton had made tentative inquiries towards hearing if another vessel were for sale locally, but there was none; and he dared not entertain the idea of chartering a ship—there was not only the expense of necessary private bribes to her master and mates, but the risk of being betrayed and forced to attempt a hasty getaway. Not only was Zanzibar a useful place to have his headquarters, but he had a wholesome dread of its efficient and British-controlled police.

As Milverton still puzzled over the problem, his pen idle in his hand, the door opened and his Zanzibar servant entered with that day's copy of the local newspaper. More for something to distract his mind than from any great interest in its contents, Milverton unfolded the sheets and glanced over the headlines. There seemed nothing that he specially wanted to read, and he was about to toss the paper aside when something caught his eye. Under the paragraph headed " Shipping News " he saw, among the list of arrivals in port that morning:

" *S.S. Chiwi*. Ex. Beira."

Milverton jumped to his feet, delight written on his heavy features. " So she got away! " he exclaimed to the empty room. " Someone—probably Jake who sent me that cable—has dispatched her here for orders, knowing that the wires were down. He's not such a fool as I was beginning to think. I wonder what she's brought in the way of legitimate cargo," he added with a chuckle, " for Jake 'ud arrange an ostensible reason for her coming here. Anyway, when she's discharged she can run down to Madagascar in ballast, and spring that waiting consignment across to the coast before the time-limit expires."

Milverton peered again at the newspaper through his

horn-rims. " Came in this morning," he commented.
" I wonder why Bowler hasn't been to see me before now.
Maybe, though, he got pinched, and Jake's fixed with
someone else to bring her along.

" Shall I go down instead? No, I might be recognised,
and the less direct connection I have with the *Chiwi* the
better." He turned to the desk, seized a piece of paper,
and scribbled a note. " Abdallah! " he shouted.

The servant entered.

" Go down to the water-front," Milverton ordered,
handing over the note, " and find somebody going out
to the *Chiwi* who'll take this aboard. And when you've
done so don't hang about or answer any questions—come
straight back here, see? "

Carmichael glanced again at the address which headed
the note that Derek had brought. " Easy to find, anyway,"
he commented. " One of those buildings on the main
street. I suppose I'd be wise to see what the fellow wants;
I'd be a fool to miss making contact with a possible
shipper."

" Meanwhile, shall I carry on here? " asked Derek.

" Yes. And when the holds are clear, if any of the
crew want to go ashore you can let 'em, for we shan't
start loading again before to-morrow at the earliest."

Carmichael landed at the steps and threaded his way
through the many-coloured crowd towards his destination. As he neared it, a sudden remembrance struck him.

" Dash it," he muttered, " I don't even know the chap's
name—the fool only signed his initials. I've half a mind
—— Oh, well, as I'm so close I'll go on and have a look
at the place anyway."

He reached it. The heavy carved door stood ajar, and
on the wall of the passage just inside was a board bearing

the painted names of the various tenants. Carmichael ran his eye down them.

"This must be the fellow," he muttered, remembering the letters "C.M." "'No. 5. Mr. Claude Milverton, General Agent.' Hmm, might mean anything; like Charity, that description might cover a multitude of sins! Well, here goes," he added, as he began to mount the stairs.

He found the door marked "5," and rapped. In response to a voice inside he entered.

"Yes, what can I do for you?" asked the man at the desk.

"This came from you, I believe," Carmichael replied, producing the note.

The other started. "Why yes, it did. But how did you come to receive it?"

"It's addressed to me," Carmichael retorted. "I'm master of the *Chiwi*."

"The deuce you are! What's happened to Bowler?"

The name struck a chord of memory in Carmichael's brain. He had heard it before—yes, it was the name of her former skipper, now languishing in the prison at Beira. Instantly he realised two things; firstly, that this man Milverton must be unaware of the *Chiwi's* capture and change of ownership, and secondly, that he was connected in some way with the smuggling racket. The knowledge promptly put him on his guard.

"Bowler's in jail and likely to stop there some years," he replied after a barely perceptible pause.

"The deuce he is! Well, serve the beggar right, people who make blunders and get caught must pay for it. So you've brought the *Chiwi* up here instead. Good job she got away; I suppose that last consignment had been landed when they snaffled it."

" Yes, they got the lot," came Carmichael's cautious reply.

" I had a cable from Jake telling me as much. Well, I'm glad he had the sense to send you up here, for there's an urgent job waiting. You know Diego Suarez, this end of Madagascar? "

" Never been there yet," Carmichael said, wondering how much more of the beans Milverton was going to spill.

" Well, you're going there now, and the quicker the better, for there's a consignment that wants shifting without loss of time. Sam Took'll meet you on arrival and give you the latest dope about the movements of that infernal Portuguese patrol-boat, and tell you the safest spots to run your cargo ashore. And now you've got your instructions you'd better get back aboard."

" Not a bad idea," Carmichael commented, feeling that the play was finished and the moment for a showdown had arrived. " Thanks for the pretty story; now you've done with flapping your tongue, let me tell you one. You're barking up the wrong tree. The *Chiwi's* mine. I bought her when she was auctioned after capture by the Portuguese, and I know nothing of ' Jake ' or any other of the dirty dogs you mention. Got all that? Good. Now I'll be off, and leave you to practise kicking yourself for not making sure of the facts first."

Milverton's jaw sagged and he sprang to his feet, his eyes glaring behind their lenses.

" I wouldn't start a rough-house if I were you," Carmichael advised. " I'm in pretty good trim, and you're soft and fat."

With an effort Milverton gained control of himself and sank back into his chair, silently cursing himself for his indiscretion. But his active brain told him that the bad slip might still be remedied. Skippers of coasters were not noted for high moral principles, and this chap, in shirt and trousers soiled from his morning's work, was unlikely to be different from any other. The extra expense was a drawback, but as he already knew too much he must be chartered to do the job, with a good bonus added to ensure that he kept his mouth shut.

"Of course I'm not going to start what you call a 'rough-house', " Milverton began. "Er—sound business is not conducted on these lines, let me tell you. I was only surprised at what you tell me. A pity you didn't speak earlier. However, things being as they are, I'm open to make you an attractive business offer."

He made it, and paused expectantly.

"Want an answer?" Carmichael asked.

"Of course."

"Then the answer is that I hope to hear very shortly that you are occupying a cell next to your late employee, Bowler. So now you know. G'bye."

Before Milverton could make any reply Carmichael had left the room and slammed the door behind him.

When he returned aboard Derek greeted him with a question. "Well, did you find him? What did he want?"

"Something I wasn't prepared to do," Carmichael grinned in reply. "I hadn't been in the place five seconds before I began to smell a rat. I lay low and the rat came out of its hole, and an ugly-looking brute it was! That fellow's either the boss or one of the prime movers in this vessel's recent activities." He went on to give an account of his interview with Milverton.

"What next?" Derek asked. "Going to tell the police?" He nodded towards the town beyond the strip of blue water.

Carmichael gave a shrug. "Wouldn't do much good.

There were no witnesses, and if questioned he'd deny ever having seen me. It would be just my word against his. And even if they believed me they couldn't charge him with anything—he's done nothing against the laws of this island. But when we get back to Beira I shall give the Portuguese the tip. After all it's their business, not ours.

" So you've finished discharging," he went on, changing the subject. " Did any of our lot want to go ashore when they knocked off? "

" About half a dozen. You'd said they could, so I told them that was all right. Yoruba was one, with a friend of his from your old crew, and the others were some of the new lot that were signed on. I expect they're all deep in that rabbit-warren of a bazaar by now, chaffering with the Indian stall-keepers."

Derek was right in his surmise where five of them were concerned, but the sixth had taken quite a different route. In fact he was making towards the very building which Carmichael had so recently left.

His footsteps slowed as he came in sight of it, and several times he paused to look at the contents of some stall that he was passing, and to cast a keen glance up and down the street. Finally, having made sure that there was nobody in the vicinity who appeared interested in his movements, he reached the doorway and entered. Soundlessly he ascended the stairs on his bare feet, and gently tapped on the door of No. 5.

CHAPTER SIX

THE "CHIWI" SAILS

AFTER the door had slammed behind Carmichael, Milverton indulged in a fit of cursing that was both fluent and picturesque. Why, he asked himself, had he been such a fool as not to make sure of his man before talking as he had? The arrival of the *Chiwi* at the anchorage had put a preconceived idea into his head, and nullified his usual caution.

Instead of being better, things were worse than they had been. He was no nearer to securing a ship to run that waiting consignment, for he could not hear of any vessel for sale, either locally or along the mainland coast, and he dared not risk chartering in the open market. To this was added the apprehension of what his recent visitor might do with the information he had blurted out. A vessel must be secured and the fellow's mouth effectually closed before that consignment could be run, but what steps to take towards arranging these two matters he had at present no idea.

Pacing up and down the room he formed and discarded several theories. Either they were impracticable or else too likely to miscarry and involve him in an unpleasant situation. Yet he would have to decide soon on his course of action, for time was vitally important and he could not afford to wait.

Presently Milverton became conscious of a repeated tapping at his door. He growled an order to enter.

" Hallo, who the blazes are you? " he demanded, as he eyed the native who had padded in.

A grin slowly spread across the other's black face.

Milverton looked more closely at him. " Why, it's Tambo, who was second engine-boy of Bowler's old crew! How did you get here, Tambo? " he went on in Swahili.

" In the *Chiwi*, master, working as fireman under a Cape-boy from the south. A fireman—me! " he added scornfully.

" But how did you manage to get free? I thought . . . Here, you'd better tell me what happened, right from the beginning."

Tambo did so, speaking of the capture of the *Chiwi* as she was approaching a spot that was thought to be safe, of how she was escorted into Beira, and how the white members of her crew had been clapped in prison.

" What about you—didn't they shove you there too? " Milverton asked.

Tambo's grin widened. " We all said we knew nothing about anything, that we were innocent black people who had been forced to do what we were ordered once we had signed on. So the police just cursed us and let us go."

" And after that? "

" We went to the white man whom you call Jake, and he gave us money for food and told us to keep in touch with him. Presently we heard that the *Chiwi* had been sold and that her new owner wanted hands to get her off the sand where the great storm had blown her and to serve as her crew afterwards. We went, and he chose seven of us."

Tambo paused to fumble beneath his tattered shirt. After a good deal of contortion he produced a crumpled and extremely dirty envelope. "Just before we left the white man Jake gave me this."

Milverton opened the note and read it eagerly. Presently he tossed it down on the desk with a grunt—it told him little more than what he already knew.

There was silence for a minute, and then Tambo spoke again.

"I must go now, master, or the others who are not of our party may begin to ask where I am. Have you any orders for us?"

Milverton slowly shook his head. "No, I don't think so." Then a passing thought struck him and he added, "Any idea what ports the *Chiwi's* calling at on her return voyage?"

It was Tambo's turn to reply in the negative.

"No matter, it's not important," Milverton commented. "But where you're going is sure to get round the ship before you sail, and if you find out, let me know. Now you'd better clear off, for I've other things to think about."

Tambo did not forget. Though he had no further opportunity to come ashore himself, he found a means of communication. On the evening of the following day Milverton's servant brought him a torn scrap of paper, which he said had been given him by one of the boatmen down by the water-front. It bore four names written in Arabic characters, no doubt by the boatman himself, but Milverton guessed at once who had dictated and sent them.

Three of the names did not interest him, but one in the middle riveted his attention. Minute after minute passed and Milverton stood motionless, his brain working rapidly; then with a slight jerk of his head he came to a decision.

Cable communication with Beira might still be difficult, but there were other places that were not so hampered. Milverton plucked a telegraph form from the rack beside him and began to write, pondering over each word. When it was finished he took it to the office himself and dispatched it. The man to whom it was addressed would not fail, he knew, to decipher the hidden meaning under the commonplace phrases, and could be trusted to act with promptitude and decision.

He left the post office feeling far more cheerful than he had for some time. Once more he went over the plan in his head, and could find no flaw. With a brisk step he made his way back, pausing only at a certain office to enter and inquire when the next liner belonging to the French-owned Madagascar service was likely to call on her way south.

Meanwhile, aboard the *Chiwi*, the work of loading was nearing completion. It was a job that needed careful planning, for instead of a large consignment there were four separate ones, each for a different place. The stuff for the most distant port, Beira, had to go at the bottom of the holds, while that for Ibo, the first call, and Mabina, the tiny spot that Derek had had to go ashore to verify, had to be at the top and easily available. Without constant supervision, the native stevedores were only too prone to reverse the order.

At length the last lighter was emptied and towed away. The hatch-covers were replaced, tarpaulins spread, and wedges holding the metal strips in place hammered home in their brackets. Derrick-booms were unshipped and brought fore-and-aft, and the vessel made ready for sea. Carmichael received his clearance-papers, and at sunrise the following day steamed away from Zanzibar.

The distance to Ibo, her first port of call, and situated near the northern end of the coast of Portuguese Mozambique, was nearly four hundred sea miles—approximately three days' steaming at the *Chiwi's* moderate speed.

The weather was clear, and the sun shone down upon a sea that was calm and intensely blue, while by night the indigo vault above was spangled with a million stars of a brightness never seen in northern latitudes. Under Half-crown's care the engines were running smoothly and without any hitch, and the varied members of the native crew seemed to have settled down together into a cheerful routine. Derek, who had got over the initial strangeness of his new job, felt that life was good, forgetting that where things are too perfect there is usually trouble not far away.

The first stopping-place, the little port of Ibo, came in sight at length, its buildings standing white against the encircling green of the coconut palms, and flanked by two ancient Portuguese forts. Derek, watching it grow larger as they approached, saw that the town stood on a small island separated from the mainland by a narrow channel, and that the anchorage was an open one, inadequately protected by a long shoal. Under Yoruba's pilotage the *Chiwi* drew in to her berth.

Though the amount of cargo to be discharged was not great, the job took longer than it need have done, and Derek was not sorry when the hatch-covers were at last replaced. At first sight Ibo had looked an attractive spot, but closer acquaintance with it had made him change his mind. As regards variety of population it resembled a small edition of Zanzibar, but instead of being picturesque and colourful the town gave him the impression of being merely squalid.

"What's our next port of call like?" he asked Carmichael when the *Chiwi* was once more at sea and Ibo had sunk below the horizon astern.

"Mabina? To tell the truth, I really don't know," Carmichael replied. "Though I've passed along this coast a score of times, I've never actually been there. In fact, I doubt if one vessel a year puts in there, excepting, of course, Arab dhows."

"Hardly a port at all," Derek commented, feeling a sort of personal interest in the place, since it had been over its identification that he had gone ashore in Zanzibar to interview the sender of the small consignment they carried.

Carmichael nodded. "Yoruba's been there—I've yet to strike a spot on the coast where he hasn't!" he went on. "He tells me it consists of about half a dozen buildings all told, mostly trading-stores dealing with produce carried down on natives' heads, or by dug-out canoe, from the interior. It's not situated on the coast itself but a couple of miles up a tidal river, which we'll probably find well-sown with shoals."

"Doesn't sound too good," Derek remarked.

"No. But Yoruba says there's a channel quite deep enough for a vessel of our draught, and that he knows it well. So with care we should have no difficulty. After all," he added with a shrug, " one's got to take the rough with the smooth in coaster work; there wouldn't be a living in it if we touched only at larger ports, for the big ships belonging to the well-known freight lines would cut us right out of business."

One afternoon, a couple of days later, when Derek came on deck after spending a " watch below " in his bunk, he saw that they must be nearing their destination. The *Chiwi* was running closer to the coast than she had been, and the low mangrove-fringed shore to starboard was

clearly visible. Though the sky was fairly clear the sea
was choppy, having been roughened by the head-wind
against which the vessel had been steaming for the last
twenty-four hours.

Derek ascended to the bridge to find Yoruba at the
wheel and Carmichael leaning over the rail studying the
coast-line that stretched ahead. The latter glanced over
his shoulder as he heard Derek's step.

" We should have been off the mouth of that river by
now," he said, " but that infernal head-wind we've been
pushing against has held us back." He turned an eye
towards where the westering sun was visible, half ob-
scured by some rolling clouds. " Yoruba reckons we
ought to sight it any time now, and I hope to goodness
we do, for I wasn't reckoning on getting there after nightfall."

An hour passed without any sign, and Carmichael's
face grew anxious. The cloud-veiled sun touched the
horizon. Almost at the same moment Yoruba called and
pointed.

He had spotted a break in the low shore. It was the
mouth of the river they were seeking.

Carmichael straightened himself. " All right, Yoruba,
you know the place and I don't, so I'll leave the pilotage
to you. But for heaven's sake don't run us on some
shoal."

" If Allah wills we shall not touch sand," Yoruba
replied, and turned the wheel a couple of spokes. The bow
of the *Chiwi* turned slightly off her previous course.

Night comes swiftly in the tropics, and before the vessel
had covered half the distance towards the river mouth
darkness was descending like a veil. Carmichael rang
down for half speed, and peered anxiously into the gloom.

He was in two minds whether to allow Yoruba to carry

on or to give the order to stand out to sea. He did not want
to waste several tons of coal in steaming round all night
and returning to the same spot at dawn. On the other
hand if the *Chiwi* grounded on a shoal, while trying to
enter there might be unpleasant consequences, for the sky
did not look too good and the glass was falling slightly.

When he mentioned his inclination to turn and stand
off until morning, Derek felt that it would probably be a
wise decision, but Yoruba protested volubly.

" No, master, it is easy, very easy. Many times have I
been here. See, it is thus. Close to the lip of the river's
mouth nearest us lies a very small island with five coconut palms growing on it—we shall come to it presently.
Once past it, on the opposite side and higher up the river
we shall see the lights of cooking-fires, where there is a
village of black heathen." Being half an Arab and a
Moslem, Yoruba always referred to negroes in this scorn-
ful way. " By keeping the island behind and the fires in
front," he continued, " we shall safely pass the sands and
shallows. Off the village we can anchor, and steam up to
the stores at Mabina when the sun rises."

Carmichael gave way. Yoruba had never let him down
yet, and there was no reason why he should do so now.
At slow speed the vessel moved onwards.

Though the night had now fully come it was by no
means pitch dark. Stars were shining down brightly
between the clouds, and the sea glimmered with phos-
phorescence. The tiny islet with its five wind-bent palms
loomed up and slid slowly past to starboard. The spokes
of the wheel turned as Yoruba brought the vessel's stern
into line with it, while Carmichael and Derek peered into
the darkness to pick out the lights which should now be
visible.

But not one distant gleam of village cooking-fires

greeted their eyes. Carmichael reached for the handle of the bridge telegraph and rang the engines to dead slow. "Where's your village?" he demanded of Yoruba. "There's not a glimmer to be seen."

"I cannot understand it, master. The village is yonder"—he waved a brown hand towards the darkness—"and never before have I known their fires fail as a mark."

"Well, they've done so now. Put her hard over and we'll stand out to sea again."

As Yoruba was reluctantly about to obey, Derek gave an exclamation and pointed. Slightly to port of the direction on which the bow was bearing had appeared several distant pinpoints of flickering flame.

Yoruba's teeth gleamed in the glow from the binnacle as he grinned with satisfaction. His knowledge of the local conditions was being vindicated. "No need to turn back now, master," he said triumphantly as he brought the *Chiwi's* bow into line with the winking lights, "did I not say we should see them. Soon, very soon now, we shall be inside the river."

Carmichael's only reply was a grunt. He began to wish that the lights had not become visible at that moment, but as they had appeared he felt reluctant to insist on his order to put out again. "All right, carry on," he said, resting his hands on the rail and frowning in the direction of the distant beckoning points.

CHAPTER SEVEN

TROUBLES NEVER COME SINGLY

WITH her propeller revolving only sufficiently to keep
steerage way on her, the *Chiwi* steamed slowly onwards.
From time to time the voice of one of Carmichael's old
hands, who had been stationed forward, rose through the
still night air, chanting the soundings in the Swahili
tongue. So far the depth of water was satisfactory, and
Carmichael began to feel more at ease.

Suddenly the native's voice rose a couple of octaves as
the soundings abruptly shallowed. Carmichael put out
his hand to the telegraph, but before he could jerk the
handle to " stop " those aboard felt the vessel check and
there was a faint scraping sound from beneath her
bottom. It lasted for a moment and then she slid free,
but there was no doubt that she had touched ground.

Carmichael turned his head to glare at Yoruba. " I
thought you knew every inch of the channel," he growled
sourly.

" Yes, master, I do. That must have been cast up since
I was last here. But there is good water under us now."

" I was a fool to attempt coming in," Carmichael
muttered to Derek who stood beside him. " I'd like to
anchor and stop where we are, but we must be right on
the river bar, and if the wind got up we'd be in for a
proper dusting. At the same time, whatever Yoruba may
say, I'm not going on blindly. Get one of the boats
lowered, take the leadsman and a couple of hands to row,
and plot out the channel ahead."

Derek obeyed, and presently he was afloat on the sullen black water, surrounded by a halo cast by the lantern which had been brought in order to reveal his whereabouts to those aboard the coaster. From his low level he could hardly see those flickering fires ashore, and they seemed to have leaped back an immense distance, but an occasional glimpse enabled him to keep his right bearing.

The boat moved forward in silence except for the click of oars and the plop of the lead, while the *Chiwi* crawled after her. At first the soundings were satisfactory and some progress was made, but presently shallower water was encountered, and the real work of exploring began.

First to one side and then the other Derek steered the boat, while the hand kneeling in the bow probed for greater depths. But nowhere could they be discovered. The channel they had been following had apparently ceased to exist, and though the *Chiwi* only drew a few feet, her way seemed completely barred.

After half an hour of fruitless search Derek picked up the lantern and waved it, a signal to Carmichael that he was returning alongside.

" We seem to have run into a regular pocket," he reported when he had stepped aboard, " a sort of long and twisting basin surrounded by shoals, without any practicable outlet that I can discover."

" Then we'll just have to make the best of it and anchor," Carmichael replied. " We've already bumped over one shoal, and with the tide falling as it is we'd never get back across it. Luckily we must be well inside the bar by now, so unless the weather blows up really bad we should be fairly well placed."

Carmichael turned his head towards where Yoruba stood, about to make a cutting remark about the result of his pilotage, but the man, who was still grasping the wheel-spokes, was looking so hopelessly downcast that the comment died on his lips.

Though the words were unuttered, Yoruba must have guessed what Carmichael was thinking. "There are shoals where none should be," he protested. "Allah has changed the whole bed of the river, and who shall find fault with his deeds?"

"I should have put it down to Sheitan rather than Allah!" Carmichael pointed out. "More likely, however, the village whose fires you were using as a guide has moved to another site."

Yoruba shook his head. "If they had moved I should have heard. It is the river that is bewitched."

Carmichael turned back to Derek with a shrug. "We'd better turn in and get some sleep. At full ebb it's possible we may ground, but luckily the bottom's soft. There's nothing we can do till morning, when we shall have both light and a rising tide. The weather's the only anxiety, but we must hope there's no great change."

That hope was justified. The wind dropped about midnight and was followed by gentle rain which gradually died away. When Derek and Carmichael came on deck at dawn they found the ship shrouded by drifting mist, which thinned and thickened periodically under the pressure of a light off-shore breeze.

"Nice spot we've fetched up in," Carmichael remarked, indicating several low hummocks of mud whose leaden backs were not yet covered by the slowly rising tide. "However, high water's not far away now, and we'll find a way out even if we have to return as we came. Hope this fog will have cleared by then."

As he spoke a puff of wind temporarily dispersed the mist, revealing the river banks. Derek glanced towards the spot from which those fires had gleamed the previous night, but he could see no signs of any village. And then he caught sight of the huts, standing above the bank at a considerable distance to the right.

Carmichael had also observed the fact. " Makes one begin to agree with Yoruba that the river's bewitched," he remarked with a grin. " Then it certainly wasn't the village fires we saw. I wonder why not—they should have been visible. What was it we did see then? "

" Perhaps they'd been burning a patch of jungle for cultivation," Derek suggested, " and we saw the dying flames."

" Not in mangrove swamp," Carmichael replied, shaking his head. " Well, we may learn one day, not that it matters very much now," he added, and as he turned away the mist closed down once more, shrouding the bank from sight.

Time passed. The rising tide submerged the shoals that had been partially visible, and Carmichael felt it would not be long before he could set about extricating his ship. Meanwhile, down below, Half-crown was busy getting up steam after a night of banked fires.

From out of the mist came the unexpected click and splash of oars, and a boat emerged to sight. It was being pulled by a couple of natives, while two white men were sitting in the stern. As it approached, one of them stood up, cupped his hands to his mouth, and hailed.

" Steamer ahoy! "

Carmichael hailed back, wondering, as Derek also did, who they could be.

" Heard a ship tried to get in las' night and found trouble, Cap'n, so we've come down from Mabina to give a hand," said the second white man.

" Very good of you," Carmichael replied. " But don't

you bother, I can steam clear easily enough when the tide reaches its full."

"Don't need us, eh? Okay, then we'll push off again." The man made a movement as if to give an order to the native rowers and then paused. "I say, Cap'n, if you're steamin' up to Mabina you can give us a lift. Save pullin'."

Carmichael agreed. He disliked strangers aboard, especially when about to engage in a ticklish job, but he felt it would be ungracious to refuse after they had taken the trouble to come and offer assistance. The boat slumped against the *Chiwi's* plates, and the two white men scrambled aboard.

"My name's Campbell," said the man who had done the hailing, as the two advanced to where Carmichael and Derek stood. "And this is Gould. Gosh! It's fine to run up against British people to talk to, Cap'n—at Mabina they're mostly dagoes and fellows of that kind." For some minutes he chattered on, while Carmichael replied absently, for his eye was on the rising tide. Presently Campbell noticed his preoccupation, and nudged his silent partner.

"I guess we're in the way. We'll take a stroll round a bit, Cap'n, if you've no objection, and leave you to carry on."

Carmichael was relieved to see their backs, for it was time to make final arrangements. Derek received his orders, and presently, as he was passing the open door leading down to the engine-room, he encountered Gould.

"I shoved me 'ead in there a minute back, mister," he remarked with a jerk of his thumb, "and seemingly there was a row goin' on down below among them niggers. You'd best 'ave a look."

Wondering what was the matter, for he could hear

nothing going on, Derek did so. From the top of the iron
ladder everything seemed normal, but to make sure he
descended to where Half-crown stood by the gauges,
keeping an eye on his little gang of stokers.

"Quarrel? No baas, no quarrel here," Half-crown
replied to Derek's question, a puzzled look on his face.
Then he added, "What those strange white men come
aboard? One put head in at top of ladder just now."

Derek explained about the visitors. "It was the man
who looked in here who told me of trouble below," he
went on.

"Then he one liar!" Half-crown retorted. "I see his
head, he shout somethin' and pop out again. I not hear
so ask those what he say"—Half-crown indicated his four
firemen—"but they say, 'know nothing,' and look stupid.
This lot we took on at Beira poor stuff—not like gang on
my las' ship."

"Oh well, as there's nothing wrong here I'll be going
up," Derek commented. "We shall be moving in a few
minutes, I expect. You've a full head of steam?"

"Ya, baas, plenty steam."

Derek nodded, and turned to grasp the iron hand-
rail of the ladder. As he did so, from above came a sudden
hooting roar of sound, and as abruptly it stopped.
Someone had pulled the lanyard of the steam siren
attached to the funnel. Derek gave a startled exclamation
—what was the reason for that unexpected and urgent
hoot?

He had little chance to speculate. As the roar of the
siren struck upon their ears, the four stokers dropped
their shovels and slices, and flung themselves on Half-
crown and himself.

The attack was so sudden that Derek had not time to
get in even one blow before he went down with two lusty

natives on top of him. But though the concussion with the iron deck-plates knocked half the breath out of him, his assailants were not to have it all their own way. Doubling his knee he managed to give one of them a shrewd blow in the stomach which made the fellow gasp, and get in a half-arm punch with his fist on the jaw of the other. Neither released their hold, however, and though Derek struggled furiously he felt himself being overpowered.

Half-crown was more lucky. Not only did the two who had attacked him fail to get as good a grip, but as he fell his hand came in contact with a heavy $\frac{7}{8}$-inch spanner that lay on the plates. Grasping it by the handle, he lashed out savagely at the nearest head. There was a crunching thud, and one of his assailants went limp. With a heave he flung off the other man, who promptly leaped back out of the swing of the steel spanner. Ignoring him for the moment, Half-crown regained his feet and sprang to help his white companion.

Derek felt himself suddenly released, for those who had got him down, seeing they were about to be taken in the rear, jumped back out of danger. Next moment the three of them were scrambling in panic flight up the ladder, leaving their fourth member lying motionless on the plates.

Derek got up, his eyes alight with anger at this sudden and inexplicable onslaught. He jerked out a question to Half-crown, but the Cape-boy was equally puzzled as to the reason for this violent mutiny. Then Derek caught sight of the prone body of the man whom Half-crown had laid out. " Who's that? " he muttered, rubbing the bruised back of his head.

Half-crown nonchalantly turned the body over. " It is Tambo," he remarked.

The man who had secretly visited that house in Zanzibar had got more than he bargained for. The $\frac{7}{8}$-inch spanner had effectually smashed his skull.

Derek shook himself, thankful to feel that the dizziness caused by his violent contact with the iron floor was passing off. Whatever the cause of the unprovoked attack, he must see Carmichael at once. "Stop here, Half-crown," he said, "while I go up and——"

A voice from above interrupted his words. The stranger who had been introduced as Gould was standing at the top of the iron ladder leading to the deck, with the three firemen who had fled for safety clustered behind him.

"Hey, mister, you'd best come up quiet and bring that Cape-boy with you. You'll get pepper if you doesn't. Your skipper's safe in the bag as the sayin' is, along o' the hands who didn't once belong to our old crew, and the ship's ours again."

The words gave Derek the clue and he began to understand what was happening. With the exception of Yoruba, Half-crown, and one or two others, he knew that most of the hands whom Carmichael had taken on at Beira had been members of the *Chiwi's* crew prior to her capture by the Portuguese. The two strangers who had appeared out of the mist with their offer of "help" must therefore be connected with the recent liquor-smuggling racket, and during their apparently innocent stroll round the ship had made brief but effective contact with these natives. Derek realised now why Gould had spoken to him about a fictitious row in the engine-room; no doubt the idea was to separate him from Carmichael and make individual capture easier when the signal, that unauthorised hoot on the siren, was given. Their ultimate object, however, still remained a mystery.

As these thoughts flashed through Derek's brain the man Gould began to descend the ladder, his three followers close behind.

After the recent rough-and-tumble Derek was in no mood to surrender tamely, for his temper had been thoroughly roused. He glanced around for an effective means of resistance.

At the moment when the siren had hooted one of the mutineers had been using a fire-slice and had instantly let go of it to obey the signal. Its long handle still projected from the open door of the furnace, while its blade among the coals was now red-hot. As the party reached the foot of the ladder, Derek plucked it forth by the handle and charged.

A red-hot fire-slice is a terrifying weapon. White man and black turned to scramble back hastily by the way they had come, but not all of them escaped scot-free. Though Gould managed to dodge its swing, the glowing blade descended with a smack on the stern of one of the mutineers. There was a puff of smoke, a reek of burnt flesh, and an appalling yell. The routed party went up the ladder a good deal quicker than they had come down, Gould's language meanwhile being almost as hot as the slice he had fled from.

Derek was not to remain long in enjoyment of his victory. A fresh figure appeared above, that of Campbell, the other visitor who had arrived in the row-boat. He carried a pistol in his hand, and as he surveyed the scene a smile flickered across his face.

"Very commendable, young man, but not very wise," he called down in a voice much more refined than Gould's. "You see, it's not going to do you the slightest bit of good. So come along up like a good boy and bring that other fellow with you. You see this pistol? If you're not started by the time I count ten, I shall have to use it. Understand?"

Derek cursed under his breath. Neither his trusty fireslice nor Half-crown's spanner could reach that smiling figure at the top of the ladder, and to try a rush would be asking for a shot. Campbell began to count. He reached "ten" and raised the pistol. A report rang out as Derek dodged round the condenser and Half-crown dropped behind a pile of coal, and the bullet flattened itself harmlessly against a piece of ironwork.

Derek peeped out, and the man above, who had taken a couple of steps downward, promptly fired again. Derek ducked back into cover, cursing the fact that he had no means of retaliation. The enemy meant business and, though it might be postponed, there could be only one outcome. He hated the idea of tamely submitting, yet it seemed inevitable. As he hesitated, trying to make up his mind to it, there came an unexpected development.

CHAPTER EIGHT

DEREK MEETS AN OLD ACQUAINTANCE

WITH Gould standing watchful behind him, Carmichael had appeared at the door above the top of the ladder.

Campbell, half-way down the steps, turned his head.

" Oh, there you are, and about time, too, if you don't want that mate of yours hurt," he remarked. " You'd better tell him to be a good lad and come to heel as he's been told."

Carmichael nodded, and called out Derek's name. " Chuck it and come up," he ordered. " These blighters have got the ship, and we must make the best of it."

Derek heard, and peered cautiously from his cover. He saw that Campbell had lowered his pistol and was leaning against the iron hand-rail, smiling as if he were watching a play. Feeling rather a fool, but having no alternative, Derek stepped out, while Half-crown also emerged from behind his protecting dump of coal. As they climbed up Campbell stepped aside to let them pass, and then closed in behind them. Thus escorted, they joined Carmichael and passed out on to the deck.

Derek saw that a third white man was there, keeping an eye on Yoruba and a couple of loyal natives who had belonged to Carmichael's former crew. The newcomer had arrived by a second boat, that had been lying off in the mist until the moment of action.

As Derek looked at him the picture of a past scene rose in his mind—a moonlit street crossed by a bar of yellow light and a figure sprawling on the road. He recognised the fellow as that far-from-sober ruffian whom he had helped to his feet that night in Beira.

The man answered Derek's look with a gap-toothed grin.

" 'Ullo mister, so you didn't go for to 'eed that strite tip I give you. Thought I was talking through me 'at, I suppose, and didn't take no notice. You 'ad fair warnin', so you can't blime nobody but yerself for this 'ere."

" Dry up, Bert, and get on with the job," Campbell broke in impatiently. " Take over this Cape-boy with the others," he went on, indicating Half-crown, " and find somewhere forward where you can lock 'em up. I'll look after the master and mate—there's a cabin amidships that'll do for them. Get a move on, for the tide's about full, and the sooner we shift this vessel into the deep-water channel the better."

So saying, he hustled Carmichael and Derek onwards, and thrust them into what had been the latter's cabin, securing the door firmly behind them.

Left to themselves the two prisoners looked at each other. For a couple of minutes neither said anything. Then, as often occurs when two minds are full of far more urgent things, the silence was broken by a trivial question from Carmichael.

" How did you come to be in the engine-room ? "

Derek told him of how the man Gould had inveigled him down on a false report, and of what had happened.

Carmichael nodded. " I suspected something of the sort. I suppose they wanted to get us separated and make things easier. You seem to have put up a better show than I did—they had me baled-up and helpless before I knew what was happening."

" It's the gang who used to run this ship, I gather," Derek commented.

" Obviously, from what they said. You remember that chap Milverton whom I saw in Zanzibar? He's at the bottom of all this, I'll swear, but how he's managed to pull the strings I've no idea. From what he let out he was in urgent need of a vessel to run another cargo." Carmichael made an angry gesture, striking the edge of the bunk beside him with his fist. " I was a fool not to be more on guard when those fellows turned up this morning, but such a development never occurred to me. Even now I don't understand it, for trying to regain his own vessel seems to me a mad scheme on Milverton's part."

" Why? " Derek asked.

" Because I should have thought she'd be just the ship he'd have avoided like the plague, now that her past connection with the smuggling racket has been exposed," Carmichael replied, dropping into a sitting position on the bunk and staring moodily at the opposite wall.

After half a minute's silence he spoke again. " Strikes me I've been an outsize in fools," he growled.

" Why? In what way? " Derek asked.

" Instead of telling Milverton just where he got off, I ought to have played up to him. Taken his instructions and walked out, leaving him to think I was going to do what he wanted. There'd have been none of this business then; we'd have reached Beira before Milverton discovered we'd not changed our course for Madagascar, and we'd have handed over what we knew to the Portuguese police, and left 'em to get on with it."

Derek nodded, realising that what his employer said was quite true. However, it was easy to be wise after the event, and direct action on the lines which Milverton had taken had never been anticipated.

" If I'd had time to think I'd have kept my mouth shut," Carmichael went on. " But it was enough to make anyone wild the way he seemed to take it for granted that I was as big a rogue as himself! I couldn't resist it somehow, and it never occurred to me that he could do anything about it, especially once we were out at sea. Oh well, it's no use chewing over what's been done; our worry now is what's going to happen next."

The distant ring of the bridge telegraph came to their ears, followed by the throb of the propeller. Carmichael cursed as he heard them, for the rogues who had captured the *Chiwi* were doing the very thing he himself ought to have been occupied with at that moment. Derek turned to look out of the thick glass scuttle that lighted the cabin, but found that the view had been blocked by a sack that had been hung across it from outside. Clearly their captors were taking no risk of them attempting to signal, by flicking on and off the electric-light bulb overhead, to any passing vessel there might be.

Only by the beat of the engines could they guess how the *Chiwi* was being manœuvred, and presently, when they quickened to full speed, the two in the cabin knew that the ship was now in the deep-water channel. They estimated that the vessel must be heading out to sea once more, but to their surprise half an hour later the throb ceased and they heard the anchor-chain running out.

The door opened, and Campbell entered.

"Bit stuffy in here," he remarked. "Sorry to have to keep the scuttle screwed down and a gunny-bag over it, but the reason's obvious, isn't it? Well, Cap'n, you turned down my services as a pilot, but they've come in useful after all."

Except for a shrug, Carmichael made no reply.

"No need to look glum, Cap'n—you might be a whole lot worse off. Besides, it's your own fault. You saw our respected boss, Milverton, in Zanzibar, and he made you a fair offer, but you wouldn't take it. Hence the milk in the coconut, as the saying is. Have a cigarette?" he added, producing a case from the back pocket of his trousers. " Or would you prefer a pipe? "

Campbell might be a rogue, but at least he was a genial one. Carmichael felt that to show resentment, though natural under the circumstances, would serve no good purpose. So he accepted a cigarette, and when Campbell passed the case to Derek he did the same.

" That's better, Cap'n. No point in bearing ill-will. I never do. I can see you're bubbling over with questions —why not ask 'em? Bet you're longing to know how we brought off this affair so neatly."

" Quite true," Carmichael admitted. " How on earth did you know we were calling here, and how could you possibly tell we'd fetch up amongst those shoals? "

" The answer to the first is that Milverton's about as smart as they make 'em," Campbell replied, " and there's not much he can't find out if he wants. He wired the information to me, together with instructions. I got in touch with these other gentlemen now aboard and by devious ways we managed to forgather here in time to meet you. As regards your second question—we didn't. We had several plans, but that wasn't among them. However, I flatter myself I'm not slow to grab an opportunity that's offered—I wouldn't be Milverton's second-in-command if I were."

Campbell paused to stub out his cigarette and light another.

" Gould was on the watch, and saw you when you were still far out at sea. How did he know it was the *Chiwi*, considering it was getting dusk? Because one of our late crew that you had aboard switched a light on and off in the fo'c'sle three times. You didn't see that from the bridge, Cap'n, because the scuttles face outboard, but Gould did.

" To tell the truth we never thought you'd try coming in, considering it was almost dark. But when you held on towards the river mouth we did some quick planning. You had someone aboard who knew the river, and the value of the village lights as a bearing. We legged it for that village, forced the niggers to dowse their fires, and lit others specially for your benefit. Simple, wasn't it? We chuckled as you came confidently in, and put yourself just where we could work things without undue publicity. We were even given a mist this morning, which prevented you spotting that we hadn't come down from Mabina."

" And now I suppose you reckon to use my ship for running that consignment that Milverton told me about," Carmichael put in. As the fellow seemed so keen to talk he felt it would be a good idea to encourage him. There was always a chance of his letting out something that might eventually prove useful.

" You've hit it in one, Cap'n," was the reply.

" Then it strikes me you're asking for trouble. Everybody knows about the *Chiwi* by now. I should have thought Milverton would have seen that clearly enough, and tried to obtain some vessel as unlike her as possible."

Campbell laughed. " My dear chap, grant us a little finesse. Just because everyone knows about her recent history she'd be the last to be suspected. There aren't any flies on Milverton, and he knows the value of a good spot of bluff. He wanted two things: to buy or pinch a ship somehow and to shut your mouth, and I guess he's killed two birds with one stone."

" It's one thing to pirate a vessel and another to make use of her," Carmichael retorted. " You can't enter any civilised port without questions being asked."

Campbell laughed again. " Oh yes, we can." With an outstretched finger he emphasised his points. " You're not on a regular run—you're tramping. No reason, therefore, that the *Chiwi* shouldn't turn aside for an extra lot of cargo. You're not due to turn up at Beira with what you have under hatches on any definite date, and by the time anyone begins to comment on your non-appearance and ask questions, we'll be through with the job."

" But—— " Carmichael began.

" There aren't any ' buts.' This vessel's papers are in perfect order—I've taken the liberty, Cap'n, to look them over already and make certain. Perhaps you've forgotten mentioning to Milverton that you were unknown at any Madagascar port? Good enough. *I* shall represent Cap'n Carmichael, and—let's see—yes, Gould can understudy our young friend here as mate. He's a bit older, but no matter, he won't be asked for his birth certificate! "

" You seem to have got it all taped out," Carmichael grunted sourly.

" Of course. For instance, where do you think we are now? "

" Anchored off the mouth of the river, waiting to pick up some more of your pals, I suppose."

" Quite wrong. We're anchored off Mabina, getting ready to off-load the cargo you brought. You seem surprised. Don't you see that someone's quite likely to have noticed the *Chiwi* entering the river, and if she steamed off without discharging, your consignee would promptly kick up a song, and awkward inquiries might be made? Nothing like attention to detail, Cap'n, if one doesn't want to trip up. Which reminds me, I'd better see to it," Campbell added, and turning towards the door he passed through and secured it firmly behind him.

When Campbell's steps had died away, Carmichael

looked at Derek, and for the first time since the unpleasant events of the morning a flicker of amusement crossed his face. " Rum chap, that," he remarked.

" Very," Derek agreed. " Seems to have a good conceit of himself. Comes here just for the pleasure of telling us how clever he is, and how clever he's going to be. I saw you were playing up to him, so I kept my mouth shut. He gave us a good deal of enlightenment."

" He did, and I hoped he was going to spill something that might be of real use to us." Carmichael paused, and then added wrathfully, " The cocksure blighter! Pirating my vessel and then coming down here to brag about it! Thinks he's going to get away with it, does he? Not if I can help it, but I'm dashed if I can see any way yet of getting even with him. We don't even know what he proposes to do with us."

" Keep us aboard, I suppose, while he uses the *Chiwi* for his dirty work."

" Possibly—and possibly not. He might be shy of entering a decent-sized port with prisoners aboard. We— or Half-crown and Yoruba for that matter—might find means of sending an SOS, and he'd find himself boarded by the dock police. I wish I'd remembered to ask him. If we knew his ideas about us we could plan accordingly. Anyway I hope we'll be shifted out of here soon, or we'll suffocate."

There was reason for Carmichael's last remark for the atmosphere inside the cabin was getting stifling. It was now midday. The mist had cleared and the sun was beating down with tropic violence on the iron outside. With the scuttle screwed home and the door fastened, the place was rapidly turning into an oven.

Another hour passed, while the rattle of winches and the creak of sheaves told of the consignment of cargo for

Mabina being discharged into some lighter alongside. Meanwhile the cabin became hotter and more airless, until both the captives wondered how much longer it would be possible to stick it.

At length footsteps sounded outside. The door opened, revealing the man whom Campbell had called Bert, and behind him a native-hand carrying food and water.

Though Bert was no lover of fresh air as such, the atmosphere of the cabin appalled even him. " Gosh! If there ent a fug in 'ere," he ejaculated. " 'Ot enough to melt a brass monkey. 'Ere, 'ave somethin' to drink," he went on, seizing a jug from the native and filling a couple of mugs. " Swill that down, and while you're eatin' I'll get onter Campbell and 'ave this put right."

" I hope you will," said Derek as he drank the water.

" O' course I will, mate. You acted like a gentleman that time we come across each other in Beira, and I ent one to ferget a good turn."

" There's a ventilator on the deck above and a cowl over it," Carmichael put in, pointing upwards, " but apparently it's been blocked up."

" Reckon it have," Bert agreed. " That's Campbell's doin'. 'E thinks 'isself as smart as they make 'em, 'e do, but I could tell 'im a few things 'e don't know. Look 'ere, if I leaves this door open, will you promise to stop in 'ere till I come back? "

Both Derek and Carmichael promptly agreed. Giving required parole would only bind them for a short time, and they would get some breathable air into the compartment.

Bert went off muttering, and presently angry voices were heard: Campbell rating the man for his action and the other not mincing his words in reply. But the outcome was satisfactory to those who listened, for shortly afterwards there were sounds from above, and a welcome breath of fresh air descended through the ventilator. The obstruction had been removed, and the deck-cowl turned to catch what breeze there was.

"I've put that right," said Bert when he reappeared, "and I've tole Campbell orf into the bargain. Anythin' else you want, matey?"

"Don't think so," said Carmichael, "though we wouldn't mind knowing what happens next. Are we to be kept here or dropped overboard or what?"

"Ah, now you're askin'. S'matter of fact I dunno. That there Campbell's skipper 'ere, and it's for 'im to say. But there's one thing you can be sure on—there won't be no 'eaving neither of you overboard when we're out at sea, for I'll 'ave a word to say there. I ent fergettin' the way my young friend 'ere be'aved that night in Beira."

Having unburdened himself of his words of comfort Bert left the cabin and secured the door firmly behind him.

Towards evening the noise of the derricks ceased, to be followed by the clank and rumble of the anchor-chain and the awakening throb of the engines. The *Chiwi* was leaving Mabina and making her way down-river. With the coming of darkness her bow began gently to lift and fall as she passed from placid waters to the open sea.

It was impossible for the two in the blacked-out cabin even to guess at the course she was taking, and only the note of the engines told them that she was being driven to the utmost of their capacity. The *Chiwi* might be steering straight away from the coast, or she might be running parallel with it, either northwards or southwards. It was not until the late afternoon of the following day that they were to emerge from their prison, and obtain a glimpse of their surroundings.

CHAPTER NINE

MANGROVE SWAMP

It was Gould who flung open the door. "Cummon, you're wanted on deck," he announced.

As Derek and Carmichael prepared to follow the man they heard the ting of the ship's telegraph and the propeller ceased to revolve. The stopping of the engines, combined with the summons, indicated that zero hour had come.

They emerged into the bright afternoon sunlight and glanced quickly round. Instead of being right out at sea as they had expected, the *Chiwi* had been hove-to at a point less than a mile from the coast. From horizon to horizon it stretched, long and low, the deep green of its vegetation a strong contrast to the rippling blue of the sea. The two boats with which Carmichael had replaced those lost in the cyclone had been slung out-board, and several of the native crew were waiting beside the falls.

Campbell was standing on the deck, while nearby Bert leaned against the rails. As the captives were marched up the former turned and spoke.

"If I'd had my own way I shouldn't have put in here," he remarked. "I should have stood out to sea and got rid of you by the simple method of dropping you overboard. But unfortunately Bert here is a sentimentalist—you wouldn't think so to look at him, would you?—and he started to kick up what might be described as a deuce of a stink about it."

"Ah, and 'oo wouldn't?" Bert grunted. "You can

call it what you likes with your fancy words, but I ent 'avin' nothin' to do with no murder, that's flat."

" Quite so, Bert." Campbell once more addressed Carmichael and Derek. " I've got to get rid of you somehow, and at the same time make sure that no news leaks out of recent events aboard here. This is about the loneliest stretch of coast along the whole seaboard. I'm going to chuck you ashore, and leave you to get on with it. By the time you've managed to tramp through the jungle to anywhere at all our job will be done, this vessel disposed of, and ourselves vanished completely." He waved a hand towards the out-slung boats. " Carry on, Cap'n. Bert and a couple of hands will provide you with an escort to the beach."

" What about my loyal hands that don't belong to your beastly gang?" Carmichael put in.

" I'm sending your half-bred Arab capitao and the Cape-boy in the other boat, for they're a stubborn pair and of no use to me. Gould's rounding 'em up now. As for the two or three others of your late crew—I can use 'em. They'll stop here and do what they're told, or it'll be the worse for them! I'm not going to work this vessel short-handed. Now, get a move on, Cap'n, we've wasted enough time as it is."

A couple of minutes later the boat that Derek and Carmichael had entered was being pulled away from the ship by a couple of natives, while Bert sat in the stern steering her towards the shore.

" From what Campbell said we've a good deal to thank you for," Derek said to Bert as the gap widened between them and the *Chiwi*.

" Oh-ah, tha's orlright. Always ready to 'elp a pal. I 'ad an 'int yesterday what was in 'is mind, and 's' morning I asked 'im strite out. We 'ad words."

Derek could well believe that Bert was telling the truth.

" I tole 'im I wasn't standin' for it, and offered to sock 'im one in the jaw. Mister Brainy Campbell didn't like that any, and 'e climb down. Then I went and fetched these 'ere." Bert indicated with his toe a couple of bundles of provisions which, together with a cooking-pot and a small axe, lay on the bottom-boards. " 'E wanted to send you orf with nothin', but I wasn't standin' that neither. And look 'ere, mister—I got summat else."

Bert paused to glance over his shoulder towards the other boat, containing Yoruba and Half-crown under the escort of the saturnine Gould, that followed them. Having made sure that Gould could not hear, he leaned forward and spoke again.

" 'Member that pistol o' Campbell's, what he 'ad a smack at you with down in the ingin-room? Ah. I reckon 'e's gettin' a lot too free with that there gun of 'is, and I thinks to myself, I does, that I'd feel a lot 'appier aboard to know 'e 'adn't got it, see? So I pinches it on the quiet. When you gets ashore you'll find it in one o' them bundles. Mebbe it'll come in kinder 'andy if you wants to scare orf lions and things."

Derek was about to repeat his thanks, but Bert silenced him with a gesture. " 'Old your jaw," he growled in a hoarse whisper. " Gould's over'auling us, and I don't want 'im to 'ear. I ent goin' to 'ave 'im tellin' Campbell as 'ow I took it."

By now they were close inshore, rising and falling on the ground-swell. But no possible landing-place was visible; those in the boats were faced by a wall of mangroves instead of a sandy beach. Of normal breakers there were none, for the surges rolled forward until, with a long-drawn sigh and hiss, they were lost to sight among the fantastically arched and twisted roots that rose from the very sea itself. Where the water washed around the stems they were of a sickly grey colour, but above the tidemark the contorted limbs and branches were of a reddish brown amid the metallic green foliage.

" 'Orrible! " Bert commented, glancing towards the nightmare vegetation. " The look o' them things gives me the willies. We'll 'ave to port our 'elm and coast along till we comes to a proper foreshore where you can land."

For quite a distance the two boats pulled parallel with the shore, until at last a break in the tangle and a strip of sandy beach came in sight.

" I'll run you in as close as I can ànd then you'll 'ave to wade," Bert remarked. And then, as the oars of one of the rowers touched the bottom, " Over you gets—I'll 'and you out the bundles."

Carmichael and Derek obeyed, took their kit, and then, as the rowers were about to push off, both held out their hands to Bert.

For the first time in his life, perhaps, Bert looked embarrassed, though there was nothing diffident about the grip of his horny palm. " So-long mates," he said. " I 'ates 'aving to do this, but ye see 'ow it is. Goo' luck!" He signed to the natives, and the boat drew off.

Yoruba and Half-crown had by now joined the white men on the sand, having been hove out by Gould into deeper water and far less ceremoniously. For a few minutes the four stood watching the boats recede. They reached the steamer and were hauled up, and then with a derisive toot of the siren the *Chiwi* turned and headed for the open sea.

Carmichael turned his eyes from the east towards the west, from the sea towards the land over which the sun was now rapidly sinking.

" The sooner we make a move the better. It'll be dark

before long. There should be some higher ground inland, and we don't want to spend the night here, surrounded by these mangrove swamps. I wish we had the slightest idea where we were."

Derek nodded. "Yes, we don't even know whether we're a long way north of Mabina or far to the south of it, for we got no hint of which way the *Chiwi* was steered after leaving there. However, we'll find out in time, I hope." He turned to pick up one of the bundles that had been dumped on the sand and, as he did so, Half-crown came briskly forward.

"I take um, baas." With a powerful swing, Half-crown lifted the bundle on to his shoulder, and with a gesture signed to Yoruba to take the other.

Looking at them, Derek noted with interest the effect that the present situation had had on the two men. Half-crown was cheerfully making the best of it, for in his life he had known many ups and downs and had learned to take things as they came. Yoruba however looked the picture of despondency. Having, it might be said, been born and bred at sea, and never having been more than a mile or two away from it, he viewed the prospect of leaving that familiar element with horror. Was not the hinterland a place of wild beasts and even more unpleasant black savages, dwellers in grass huts and eaters of foul foods forbidden by the Koran? With a sigh of resignation he lifted the remaining package, and with the air of a martyr going to the stake turned to follow his white masters.

The belt of sand was only a narrow one, and as the party advanced inland the firm dry surface gave place to mud. The mangroves closed in around them adding to the difficulty of making progress, for the interlacing roots tripped them at every stride and the surrounding vegetation made it impossible to see more than a few yards ahead.

The mud became deeper, and a glimpse of foul water became visible. Carmichael, who was leading, halted, his boots slowly sinking deeper as he stood.

" We'll have to hark back and try somewhere else," he said to Derek. " We seem to have struck a bad patch."

Laboriously they retraced their steps, dragging their feet out of the sucking slime. To add to their difficulties the sun disappeared behind the unseen horizon, and the darkness began swiftly to close about them.

" It looks as if we'd be wise to get back to the beach and try again in the morning," Derek commented.

Carmichael nodded in agreement. " Yes, we've no time now to hunt for a possible way round. We'd better get a move on, too, or we won't even be able to see sufficiently to find it again."

It was with thankfulness that they once more felt dry sand beneath their feet instead of clinging mud. The spot where they had been marooned was not an ideal one on which to spend the night, but at least it was better than the slimy tangle from which they had retreated.

Yoruba gazed longingly out to sea, as if by wishing he could conjure up the lights of an approaching vessel out of the darkness that shrouded it. But Half-crown was of a more practical turn of mind. Putting down his burden he began to hunt round for driftwood or anything that would burn, and almost before Derek and Carmichael had scraped the worst of the evil-smelling mud from their boots, the Cape-boy had managed to get a small fire going on the sand. Its flickering flames instantly began to make things look more cheerful, and to bring with it thoughts of something to eat.

An examination of the bundles revealed a supply of

stores that, with care, should last them for several days. One contained corned beef, biscuit, tea, sugar, and canned milk, while the other had meal for Yoruba and Half-crown. There was also a small keg of fresh water, perhaps the most important thing of all at the moment, for there was no chance of obtaining any where they were. On the top of the tins, Derek found the pistol that Bert had concealed there—a .38 Browning automatic which, on examination, was found to contain eight cartridges in the magazine. By a stroke of luck it had been fully loaded when Bert had snaffled it from Campbell's quarters.

"Will you take charge of this, or shall I?" Derek asked.

Carmichael looked up from his occupation of opening a can of bully-beef. "Ever used one before? You have? Then you'd better hang on to it yourself. I don't think we're likely to need it, but it's a comfort to know we have a weapon of some sort between us."

Seated on the sand they ate their supper by the light of the fire, while Half-crown and Yoruba on the opposite side filled themselves with some stiff porridge they had cooked. Then, their hunger satisfied, Derek and Carmichael each made a hollow in the sand to take their hips and lay down to sleep, each using as a covering one of the blankets that had been the outer wrapping of the two bundles of supplies.

They were not destined to get much sleep. As long as they had been sitting upright beside the fire, the drifting smoke had kept the mosquitoes at bay, but as soon as they lay down the enemy advanced to the attack. Of huge size and with appetites to match they swarmed out of the surrounding mangroves in millions, each intent on a fill of blood and incidentally of injecting the supplier with their stock of malarial germs.

Both Derek and Carmichael tried to defend themselves by wrapping their blankets round their heads, but after five minutes of that suffocating position they were forced to toss them aside. The fire was their only hope, and in the end they were compelled to spend the rest of the night sitting to leeward of it, feeding it with a mixture of driftwood and damp seaweed to produce a maximum of pungent smoke.

Meanwhile, to their considerable envy and annoyance, Half-crown and Yoruba snored on peacefully. The mosquitoes seemed to ignore their existence. As Carmichael cynically remarked to Derek, in Yoruba no doubt they recognised the scent of a True Believer; while in Half-crown's case it was probably that of the lubricating oil, with which, after years of messing about with engines and strict economy of soap, not only his clothes but his skin was impregnated.

As the sun rose out of the sea next morning the party gathered up their belongings and once more turned their faces inland.

This time, instead of plunging straight forward into the mangroves and the mud, they skirted along them, seeking a drier route. But it was not long before it became obvious that none existed. A halt was made for a brief consultation.

" It's my belief," said Carmichael, " that we're not on the actual coast at all. I've an idea that the spot where we landed was once an isolated sandbank thrown up by the tide, with a channel separating it from the mainland. During centuries that channel has silted up, making this bog, the roots of the mangroves creeping forward preventing it ever being washed clear again."

" Very probably," Derek agreed. " That granted, we've

no alternative but to strike straight ahead and trust to luck that we don't get swallowed up."

" Exactly. It may not be very wide—at least we'll hope not. I wish there were a decent-sized tree that we could climb to survey the ground ahead, but there's only this infernal dead-level of mangroves. Well, come on—the longer we think about it the less we shall like it."

They moved forward in silence as regards speech, but there was plenty of noise otherwise, for with each step there was a squelch, and a long-drawn viscous sucking as the foot was withdrawn. Deeper became the mud until every inch they progressed became a struggle, and it was only by grasping the contorted stems of the mangrove with their hands that they could pluck their legs from the slime. Their hearts pounded with the effort and sweat streamed from their faces, for though the sun had hardly risen, the atmosphere of the tangle was steamy with heat and damp.

The mud and the twisting roots were not their only trials, for clouds of insects, disturbed by their advance, hovered round their faces and lost no opportunity to bite and sting. Monstrous crabs peered at them with stalky eyes and raised menacing pincers, and there was always the risk of touching a snake as they clutched at the mangroves for support.

Despite the load he carried, Half-crown was keeping up with the white men, but Yoruba was falling behind. Presently he called out in a despairing voice that he could not go on.

" You've got to!" Carmichael shouted over his shoulder, while Derek, turning his head, saw that the man was buried to the waist. " Wait a minute and I'll give him a hand," he said, and struggled back to relieve Yoruba of his load and give him a pull, at the same time urging him to make an effort for himself. With a pious ejaculation to Allah, Yoruba managed to release one leg, and in doing so collapsed on his face in the mud. The sharp nip of a crab brought him upright again with a not-so-pious exclamation, and seeing there was no help for it he struggled on in the wake of the others.

They had dragged themselves through nearly a quarter of a mile of evil-smelling slime when there came a change. Derek felt his feet sinking only ankle-deep instead of plunging to mid-thigh. A few steps more, and through the interlacing vegetation he and Carmichael caught sight of an abrupt rise of ground in front. It was a long low bank about three feet high and densely overgrown, but the growth was of other species than that of the hateful mangrove, and they both gave a cry of joy as they realised they were reaching firmer soil.

Thrusting their way through the overhanging foliage, they scrambled up the bank, and paused on the crest for a much-needed rest. As Derek bent to scrape the worst of the clinging mud from his legs he saw something that made him pause and look closer.

In clambering up the little rise the feet of the party had dislodged a large piece of earth and roots, exposing stone beneath. But what intrigued Derek was that it did not look like natural rock, for the surface was square and even as though it had been dressed by hand.

Out of curiosity he tried to shift some more earth. Another chunk broke away, and Derek gave an exclamation of surprise that brought Carmichael to his side. There was no doubt about it: the stonework was part of a buried mass of ancient masonry, for the joins between the squared blocks were easily visible.

Carmichael joined in the investigation. He picked up a dead branch and levered off some more of the overlay, revealing more stones and a huge copper ring, now a mass of verdigris, attached to them.

" Didn't I say I thought that filthy bog was once an open channel? " he remarked as he straightened himself. " Two or three thousand years ago this was a wharf where ships tied up. That ring alone proves it."

" But who could have built it? Those Phœnicians who are known to have traded along the coast in B.C. times? " Derek queried.

" Phœnicians, or perhaps Persians as some think. They've left remains in a dozen known places, and probably in a hundred unknown ones like this. You ask Yoruba about them, I expect he's seen plenty." Carmichael signed to the man to approach.

Yoruba glanced with indifference at the masonry and the corroded ring. "The work of the Ancients, long before the days of the Prophet," he commented. " I have seen many such, where they tied up their big dhows that, so the tales of our ancestors tell us, moved with both sails and oars."

Derek's eyes fell again to the ancient stonework, a silent witness of the mutability of empires. Standing amid that primeval tangle it was hard to visualise the moored Phœnician galleys, the long-robed merchants chaffering on the quay while, under the crack of the overseer's whip, slaves hastened with bales of goods towards long-vanished warehouses. His thoughts were interrupted by a short laugh from Carmichael.

" Archæologists spend thousands of pounds hunting for this sort of thing, and we go and stumble on it by accident. And maybe another thousand years will pass before it's found again! Oh, well, we'd better be on the move," he ended, turning away and signing to Half-crown and Yoruba to pick up their loads.

CHAPTER TEN

THE POWER BEHIND THE SCENE

THOUGH the mud was no longer a problem, advancing inland was by no means easy, for the travellers had now to contend with the dense tropical jungle that bordered the low-lying coast. In damp and steamy shade they struggled through the tangle of undergrowth and creepers that matted the ground beneath the trees, taking it in turn to lead the way and at times hew a path with the small axe they fortunately possessed. After a couple of hours of such progress they encountered a small and sluggish stream of fresh water. The amount in the keg which had come from the ship was almost finished, and not knowing when they might strike more, they decided to halt and cook some food.

Hitherto Carmichael had made little comment on recent events, but a remark from Derek about the *Chiwi* provoked an outburst from her owner.

" They think they're going to get away with it, the crooks! " he exclaimed wrathfully. " But they won't if I can help it! All the money I have is invested in that ship. On the face of things they're on a safe wicket. They reckon to finish the job, dispose of my vessel—probably by sinking her when she's no longer safe to retain—and scatter before there's a risk of being caught, but smart plans don't always come off! I'll get my ship back yet, and have the pleasure of seeing those blighters behind bars! " he exploded savagely.

Thinking that the chances were about a million to one,

under the circumstances, Derek made the obvious comment.

"How?" Carmichael retorted. "I don't know. We don't even know where we are, much less anything else. But they're not going to get away with it if I can help it," he repeated with emphasis as he finished his meal and rose again to his feet.

As they pushed on, the going became less difficult, for they were reaching higher ground where the forest was less dense. At last they emerged from the trees on to the edge of a piece of cultivated land, and beyond the growing crops of millet and maize they caught a glimpse of the conical roofs of a native village.

"Now perhaps we'll be able to find out where we are!" Carmichael exclaimed as they threaded their way through the tall stalks towards the group of huts.

As they approached the place sprang to life. With shrill cries women called to their children and hustled them out of sight, while the menfolk picked up spears and clubs and made as if to bar the way. Seeing this unexpected development Carmichael called out to them, making friendly gestures, but obviously they did not understand what he said.

Half-crown chimed in. Although he had lived all his life in more or less civilised surroundings, he had the inborn capacity of the African for picking up a working knowledge of local dialect from men of various tribes he had come across. But his words, though understood, had as little effect as Carmichael's. Instead of lowering their weapons the villagers advanced menacingly.

"What the deuce is the matter with them?" Carmichael muttered.

The party stood their ground. The intervening distance lessened. Derek said something to his companion, who nodded. From inside his shirt Derek produced the pistol that had once been Campbell's and fired a single shot over the natives' heads.

It had the desired effect. The men retreated hastily to their starting-point and faced round once more, chattering volubly and occasionally shouting a threat.

" We seem to have struck a bad patch. Something's biting this lot, and we won't get anything out of them, so we'd better push on in the hope of striking a more friendly village somewhere," Carmichael said as the party continued their journey. He glanced over his shoulder to where Half-crown followed behind with Yoruba. " Any idea what they've got their tails up about? "

Half-crown was shrewd, moreover he had caught one or two ejaculations from the villagers that had been sufficient to give him a clue.

" They think we labour agent, baas, come to take away young men to work on *prazo* where grow sugar, or down mine."

" But supposing we had been, why this fuss? They're not forced to sign on for work if they don't want to."

Half-crown grinned. "So labour agent say, and p'aps that right near civ'lised part. But in lonely village far off in bush that diff'rent matter. 'Member, baas, agent get two-pound cap'tation-fee for each one he bring in— if he not catch man he not catch money," he explained briefly.

Derek felt that Half-crown had probably hit the nail on the head. Though he had not been long in Africa he had already learned that a good deal goes on which the world does not know about. Though slavery might officially be long dead, Africa is very old, and slow to change her habits.

It was towards evening that they struck a clearly

THE POWER BEHIND THE SCENE

defined path, one of those winding nine-inch tracks that form the highways of the bush and along which natives travel in single file. There was fresh spoor of bare feet upon it, and if followed, the track would no doubt lead to some village. The travellers promptly turned along it. Just towards sunset they entered a clearing, and saw the huts grouped at the foot of a low, isolated hill that lifted its rocky brow above the sea of forest.

" Looks a fairly large village," Derek commented. " I wonder what sort of reception we're going to get here."

Carmichael's reply was terse. " If there's any more nonsense, somebody's likely to get a broken head. We're stopping here the night, whether they like it or not."

In contrast to the earlier village, there was nothing in the way of a demonstration when the party appeared. Either the suspected labour agents did not visit that particular spot, or else the inhabitants had for some reason no cause to fear them. The people merely regarded Derek and his companions with a mixture of apathy and furtive curiosity, making no move either of welcome or otherwise.

In response to a sharp order to one of the spectators to go and fetch the headman, a dignified middle-aged native came forward. His face showed nothing of what might be passing in his mind, for it bore that inscrutable expression that a native can assume at will to hide his thoughts.

" I am Goza, the chief of this village," he said.

Carmichael nodded. " We shall camp here to-night," he said, while Half-crown translated. " Your people must bring us water, for we are weary and do not know where your water-hole lies. To-morrow we will speak to you again, for we have questions to ask of you."

There was a convenient spot on the edge of the village,

and Carmichael selected it for a camping site. The headman had made no offer of a hut, and, unless it had been a
new one, not yet occupied, the white men would not
have accepted it if he had, for a dwelling that natives have
used is likely to have too many tenants of the kind that
hop and creep. Half-crown however had no such faddy
ideas: having helped to fix up his masters' camp he
strolled off to investigate the village in search of a roof
to sleep under, and incidentally to air his sketchy knowledge of the local language.

He had hardly left the camp when he was accosted by
Goza the headman, who had been hanging around in the
hope of such an opportunity.

" Where have the white men come from, and what do
they want here? " he asked.

Half-crown always believed in a bold face and plenty
of bluff. He was not going to admit that the party were
castaways who had been dumped on the coast. To procure
information, or anything else for that matter, the headman must be duly impressed.

" Ah! " he said, " so you want to know what my
masters have come about? You may well ask! What else
do you think but to inquire into the evil things that have
been done in this village during the past year? Now
Goza, if that is your name, tell one of your people to
bring me a bowl of beer, good beer that your women
have brewed, and perhaps I can persuade the white men
to overlook some of your past misdeeds! "

The beer was brought, sampled, and approved. Having
handed back the bowl, Half-crown strolled on in search
of a hut from which he could eject the occupants. Goza
meanwhile, with anxiety now written on his face, turned
his steps towards the hill that rose behind the village.
" The Keeper of the Spirits must know of this," he

muttered as he went, " lest his curse fall upon us for keeping him in ignorance."

As is often the case, a native headman is little more than a figure-head. In the background, unseen and unsuspected, is a far greater power, and one that controls every phase of life throughout the neighbourhood. It is a control moreover that no man dare question, for to do so would bring down upon him all the relentless forces of the unseen, against which there can be no appeal.

As Goza climbed the hill his pace became slower and his manner more humble. In the gathering dusk he came in sight of the solitary hut, hung about with strange objects which he knew to be charms of terrible potency. In front of the dwelling burned a little fire, and beside it was seated a shrivelled figure wrapped in a magnificent kaross of cat-skins.

As the headman approached, Makubi lifted his head and studied his visitor with a pair of glittering eyes set in a wrinkled face. " What do you want, Goza? " he demanded. " I did not send for you."

Goza told his tale, repeating what Half-crown had said to him.

Makubi uttered a short laugh that had no mirth in it.

" These people must be very foolish if they think they will be allowed to find out things and return to report to the white man's government far away in their towns. So you have come to ask me what you are to do? "

" Yes. Does the Keeper of the Spirits wish me to drive them away? "

Makubi's calculating eyes studied the anxious headman for a minute.

" No, for they would fight and men would be killed. True, the death of a few villagers is a small matter, but some of these people might get away after all, and return a moon hence with soldiers. On the contrary, your task will be to make them stay."

" But if they will not? They spoke of questioning me in the morning and then leaving."

" That is your affair," Makubi retorted. " But, remember this. If, when the unseen powers are ready to act, they find these men are gone, then their wrath will fall upon you and no doubt they will tear your soul from your body with frightful pain, leaving it twisted into a knot! Now go, and remember what I have said."

Goza descended to the village with dismay in his heart. He never doubted what would happen if he failed to obey the orders he had received, yet how was he to control the movements of these unwanted visitors except by force, and that had been forbidden?

When, on the following morning, he was called up for questioning, Goza was even more puzzled. He had expected an inquisition into recent happenings in the district, things which men of both his own and other villages had been forced to do under the threat of Makubi's magic. Instead the white men, speaking through the mouth of their follower who only last night had warned him of the reason for the visit, asked about places he had never heard of and how far they were away. Goza felt certain that there was some subtle motive under this, and denied all knowledge of any of them—a thing he was able to do with conviction considering that it was no more than the absolute truth.

Then an inspiration came to him. Makubi had said that these men were not to leave, and their strange questions had given him an opening.

" White chiefs," he said, " though I know nothing of the places you ask about, there is a man living in a village not far away who has travelled much, even as far as the towns of the Portuguese. I will send for him, and he shall guide you to where you want to go. In the meanwhile let the chiefs stay here. See," he went on eagerly, " there is a new hut yonder that is just finished, and clean and ready for their use, and my people shall bring food and beer, and a goat shall be killed for meat. Let the chiefs stay here in comfort until to-morrow or the next day."

Carmichael glanced at Derek. " What do you think?"

" I should accept," Derek replied. " Though it will mean a short wait, we should waste far more time by wandering blindly on our own. If this chap has a guide in view it would make a lot of difference."

Carmichael nodded. " I think so too," he said, and passed on the decision to the headman.

Delighted at the success of his ruse, Goza escorted Carmichael and Derek to the newly built hut, and turned out the inhabitants of a neighbouring one to provide accommodation for Half-crown and Yoruba. He then bustled away, calling orders to his people to bring presents of food for his guests.

" They're a rum lot of beggars here," Derek commented, when he and Carmichael had settled themselves in. " I wonder what's made them change round all of a sudden like this. When we came here last night they were by no means welcoming, and now they're all on the rush to make us comfortable. At the same time they haven't lost that oddly furtive look about them which we noticed when we arrived. Although it's their own suggestion that we should remain, anyone would think we'd insisted on it, and beaten them up for objecting!"

" I don't see that it matters two hoots about their looks as long as there's no complaint about their deeds," Carmichael replied with a shrug. " Probably the bottom of the story is that they're a bit scared of us, having hardly ever set eyes on a white man before."

"Yes, I expect that's it." Derek glanced at the baskets of local produce—meal, wild tomatoes, and sweet potatoes —that had already been placed before the hut. "As you say, it's deeds that count, and these things will save us using what little's left of the stores from the *Chiwi*. No fresh meat yet, but I expect that will come to-morrow— they said something about killing a goat for us, didn't they?"

Somewhat similar comments were being exchanged in the neighbouring hut from which the occupants had been ejected to make room for Half-crown and Yoruba.

"You and the two white baas have me to thank for this, though they don't know it," Half-crown was saying. "If I hadn't talked to that headman and made him afraid of us, we should not have food and hut."

"There is only one way to treat these savages," Yoruba agreed. "My ancestors knew that, and made them fear."

Half-crown was not interested in Yoruba's fore-fathers. His mind was still running on food. "There will be meat to-morrow, good goat's meat to fill our bellies."

Yoruba shook his head sadly. "You may eat of it but I cannot: the Law of the Prophet forbids the eating of meat that is not slain in the manner ordered."

"Then there will be all the more for me," was Half-crown's comment, as he rubbed his stomach in anticipation.

CHAPTER ELEVEN

A BOWL OF STEWED GOAT

ABOUT noon on the following day, just when Derek and Carmichael were thinking of starting on their midday meal, a youth appeared at the doorway of the hut. In his hands he bore an earthenware bowl of native make, from which rose a savoury smell of stew.

" What's this? " came the question.

The lad muttered something about having been told to bring it, and to wait and retrieve the bowl when it was empty. Nervously he held out the steaming vessel.

" I suppose this is some of the promised goat," Carmichael commented to Derek as he took it. " I wish they'd sent down the raw meat so we could have prepared and cooked it ourselves, for natives' ideas of hygiene are primitive. However, the bowl looks clean and new, so let's hope it's been decently prepared."

Carmichael laid it on the floor near the entrance, and looked around for the couple of tin plates they possessed. The youth meanwhile drifted round to the back of the hut to await the empty vessel. Hardly had he gone when something else appeared near the doorway. It was a mangy and cringing native dog, attracted by the appetising smell.

" Poor brute," Derek commented. " It looks as if it had never had a square meal in its life."

" What's that? " Carmichael asked, turning his head from the hunt for plates.

Derek repeated his remark.

" Yes, they're never properly fed. Natives are cruel

beasts about animals, they leave 'em to pick up a living as best they can. Makes me wild sometimes when I see them, but what can one do? It's the ingrained custom of the country."

Unable to resist the mute appeal in the dog's eyes, Derek leaned forward and with his fingers lifted a large piece of meat from the stew. He tossed it in the direction of the starving creature, which immediately bolted with its tail between its legs.

It halted and turned, while the two men watched it with interest. " Keep still, it will come back in a minute," said Derek.

It did. Inch by inch it approached the piece of meat that lay in the sunlight, its nose sniffing eagerly. It reached the morsel, paused for a moment to make sure that no danger threatened from the silent watchers inside the doorway, and then gulped it down hungrily. Derek promptly threw it another bit which, after a nervous backward start, the dog also swallowed. The poor beast seemed to smile all over—never before in its miserable existence had it tasted such succulent food.

" Here, steady on! " Carmichael put in with a laugh, " leave some for us. Here are the plates, and a spoon to scoop it out with."

Derek ladled out some of the stew, but before either of them could begin eating their attention was drawn once more to the dog.

The satisfaction on its face had changed to agony. It was swaying from side to side, gasping and moaning. Then it turned blindly away at a staggering run, covered a dozen yards, and collapsed with a long-drawn whine. Its feet beat the air for a moment, and then its body went limp and lifeless.

The two men looked at each other across the mercifully

untouched plates of stew. "It's poisoned!" Derek breathed.

Carmichael nodded. "Thank heaven that dog turned up when it did. It's saved us from a nasty end. We must get to the bottom of this. Wait a minute, I've an idea. There was a scared look about that lad who brought it. If he didn't know definitely he had his suspicions. He's round at the back and wouldn't have seen that affair of the dog—I'll call him to take away his bowl."

Trying to make his voice sound casual, Carmichael did so. When the lad appeared he pointed to the pot, and indicated by signs and words that they had taken all they wanted and that the youth could have the rest.

As the young man stepped inside the doorway to retrieve his property Carmichael behind him, blocked his retreat. "What remains is yours," he repeated, "but eat it now."

Carmichael's knowledge of the local language was sketchy, but his words and signs were understood. The lad shrank back, turning the greyish colour that stands for pallor in a native, his eyes wide with fright.

"Ah, so you know it is poisoned! Who gave it you to bring to us?"

Silence.

Carmichael repeated the question, but got no answer. Beads of sweat appeared on the youth's forehead and trickled down his face.

"Either you will tell us, or we will force you to eat."

Still no reply.

Carmichael glanced at Derek, who neatly kicked the native's legs from under him so that he collapsed on the floor. Before he could rise, Derek was sitting on his chest. Carmichael bent over him, a piece of stew in his fingers, and deliberately forced open the lad's mouth in readiness to receive it.

"I will tell!" came from the terrified figure on the floor.

"Ah, I reckoned you'd think better of it. Who was it?"

The boy writhed. "The Keeper of the Spirits," he gasped out.

"Who's he? Hurry up or I'll push this down your throat."

In whispered sentences the lad told of the all-powerful witch-doctor whose lightest word was law, and how no man dared disobey him lest he should bring upon himself all the terrors of the unseen world and a death as agonising as it was mysterious. It was he who had decreed that the visitors should be lulled into false security by the offer of food and a hut, and then "removed" in the time-honoured fashion kept for those who might constitute a danger to his hitherto unchallenged rule. Though neither Derek nor Carmichael knew the local tongue, they were able to gather the gist of what was said.

Suddenly Derek recollected their two followers, to whom, no doubt, a portion of the same stew had also been taken. They must be warned not to eat any. With a sign to Carmichael to keep guard over the prisoner, he sprang out of the doorway and hastened towards the hut which Half-crown and Yoruba were occupying.

As he did so he saw that his warning was too late. Half-crown was staggering out of the hut, vomiting violently, while behind him was Yoruba, alarm on his brown face. As the latter caught sight of Derek he cried out: "There was death in the meat! He ate of it but I did not, not being lawfully slain—truly the Rule made by the Prophet has saved my life this day!"

Hearing the commotion Carmichael looked out, and took in the situation at a glance. He hurried across also, not forgetting to drag the prisoner with him, for there was no knowing that a use might not yet be found for him. Handing the captive over to Yoruba's care, Carmichael joined Derek in seeing what could be done for the Cape-boy.

And that indeed was hardly anything, for they had no remedies of any sort and were in complete ignorance of the nature of the poison. The one hopeful sign was the way it was being thrown up.

Spasm after spasm shook the patient. For a few moments it seemed touch and go whether he would survive, and then at last a slightly more natural tint crept back into Half-crown's grey face.

" I do believe he's got rid of it," Carmichael said with a sigh of relief. " If he'd eaten less he'd probably have been dead by now, but the betting is he gobbled it down without pausing for breath. Lots of poisons act that way—too much makes the victim bring it all up."

There was no doubt about Half-crown being better. Though utterly exhausted he appeared to have got rid of the poison, and a few minutes later he was able to speak. His first words were not complimentary to the local people, whose heads were now peering round every hut, amazement written on their faces.

There was good reason for their expressions, for such a contretemps was hitherto unknown. The dreaded witch-doctor had acted, and yet here were three of his victims unharmed, while the fourth was recovering instead of being a corpse unpleasantly tied into a knot! Moreover, the youth who was being held so tightly by the half-bred Arab was none other than their headman's favourite son, whom Makubi had insisted on being the bearer of the stew owing to the father having put forward a mild protest that morning against the contemplated murder of the guests of the village.

Now that Half-crown was able to speak again, his better knowledge of the language, coupled with blood-curdling threats, extracted a good deal more from the trembling lad than Carmichael and Derek had done.

"We're not going to take this lying down!" Carmichael exploded when it seemed that the captive had been pumped dry. "We've got to go and beat-up this witch-doctor."

"The sooner the better," Derek agreed. "Yoruba can stop here and look after Half-crown and the prisoner, who'll prove a useful hostage. Yoruba can have the axe, and he can threaten to brain the lad if those villagers dare start any funny games while we're gone."

"Come on then. Bring your pistol in case of any trouble, and this'll serve to give the beggar the beating of his life," Carmichael replied, picking up a stout stick that had been lying on the ground nearby.

The two swiftly climbed the hill, taking the narrow pathway that wound among the rocks. As they did so they caught a glimpse of several of the villagers following them, curiosity to know what next was going to happen overcoming their dread of approaching the witch-doctor's private sanctum unsummoned. Derek and Carmichael reached the brow, and saw before them the hut and its varied assortment of " charms."

In front of it squatted Makubi, brewing something in a blackened pot over a little fire. He turned his head at the sound of steps. Both fear and rage leaped into his beady eyes as he realised that for once in his evil life a plan of his had miscarried. Pulling himself together, he projected a skinny arm from the folds of the kaross that was wrapped about him, and spat out a furious curse.

The two men halted, and Makubi, feeling that his maledictions were going to prove as effective on these

white strangers as they would have been on some trembling native, felt more hopeful.   But the reason that had
made the angry pair pull up was something entirely
different. " I meant to lambast the hide off him," Carmichael muttered. " I'd forgotten he might be a withered
old stick of eighty."

" All the same, he mustn't be allowed to get away with
it," Derek reminded him, thinking of their own narrow
escape and of Half-crown's deathly spasms of sickness.

" No, he mustn't! " Carmichael agreed with an oath.
" If one of us had died I'd have found a rope somewhere
and hung him out of hand. As it is, aged or not, he's going
to sleep sore to-night! "

Makubi had seen the peering heads in the background,
and he foamed at the added insult. Those villagers too
should suffer later for their temerity! Meanwhile he
launched into the most searing curse of his repertory,
which by rights should have blasted the two white men
where they stood.

Instead they stepped forward. Carmichael caught the
old man by the wrist and jerked him to his feet, at the
same time pulling off the thick kaross that covered him.
The next moment the stick came down with a stinging
whack on his more or less unprotected body.

The cut had hurt enough, but what hurt Makubi far
more was that the outrage should have been seen by those
peering heads—those dupes who trembled at his lightest
word! With a scream of fury he whipped out a knife that
was hidden in his loincloth, and flung himself at the man
who had done it.

To avoid the sudden stab of the knife Carmichael side-
stepped, and caught his foot against one of the many
boulders that littered the hill-top. He fell, and, seeing
his advantage, Makubi was at him again like a wild-cat.

Derek's hand shot out. Gripping the old man by the neck he plucked him off before any harm was done. The knife fell from the witch-doctor's hand and he was jerked back.

For several seconds Makubi stood motionless. Then slowly his eyeballs turned upwards till nothing but the yellowed whites could be seen, his knees bent themselves beneath him, and he sank to the ground.

"Gosh! He's throwing a fit!" Carmichael exclaimed.

But Carmichael was wrong. Makubi was dead—a victim of the violence of his own consuming rage.

There was silence for a minute, which at length was broken by Derek.

"Well, that's not our doing, though if it had been it's no more than he deserved, the old poisoner! I wonder how many of the local people he's done in during past years."

"Certainly dozens and probably hundreds. However, it's not his murky past we've got to think about now, it's ourselves and the present. Strikes me we've got to look out for squalls."

"How so?"

Carmichael jerked a thumb in the direction whence those peering heads had shown themselves. Derek glanced round. There was not one of them now to be seen.

"They've bolted to tell their pals of the appalling calamity," Carmichael said sourly. "Natives are un-reasoning beggars at best, and when anything touches their superstitious fears the result is usually a riot. They'll imagine that all sorts of troubles will come now that they're deprived of the old villain's 'protection' against the evil spirits that cause droughts and floods and disease amongst their stock and themselves. Ah, listen! You can hear 'em already."

It was true. Those who had witnessed the end of Makubi were shouting the news as they ran towards the village, and the answering shouts and cries were clearly audible. The same thought leaped into both minds— what was happening to Half-crown and Yoruba who had been left among the huts? The sooner the two halves of the party made contact again the better.

Derek and Carmichael hastened down the hill. They reached the village to find it resembling an overturned ants' nest. Men and women were running hither and thither, chattering volubly, and as the two approached they scattered from their path, while children cried and babies wailed, and even the goats and fowls seemed to have caught the excitement.

Half-crown and Yoruba were sitting where they had been left, still unharmed and still in possession of the young hostage. They reported that though the village was all ends up, no one had attempted to molest them.

A few moments later a number of natives were seen approaching, Goza at their head. The little party faced round, Carmichael taking a firmer grip on his stick and Derek with his hand on the pistol he carried.

" Here, keep your distance! " Carmichael ordered, and as the natives still advanced he added sharply to Half-crown, " you can make them understand better than I can—tell 'em to sheer off, or somebody'll get hurt! "

The Cape-boy did so and the men halted. Goza gave an elaborate salute. " Chiefs, great chiefs! " he murmured in deferential tones.

This was an unexpected development, and Derek and Carmichael did not know quite what to make of it.

" Strong indeed is your power," Goza went on, " to prevail against the spells and magic of Makubi and slay him in his own place and before his own hut."

"We did not kill him," Carmichael retorted, feeling slightly bewildered at the turn of events. "Go and look —you won't find a mark on his body."

Goza ignored the statement with a smile. "Such a one does not die except from a power greater than his own. In slaying him you have lifted a great fear from us, and other villages will be glad also when they hear."

"Well, I'm—blowed!" Derek muttered. "If you're so glad about getting rid of him," he added, "why didn't you blot him out yourselves ages ago?" Half-crown translated the gist of this remark.

A look of horror at the suggestion crossed Goza's face. "How could we? The man who would dare such a thing would die horribly, torn to pieces by the evil spirits whom Makubi controlled. But now we are blameless, and no curse can fall on us. No doubt the spirits are powerless against white men," he added. "Indeed we have seen that already, or how else did they know there was death in the meat, and refuse to eat of it?"

"Yes, what about that?" Carmichael put in sharply. "This lad brought it—your son, I understand. You're as bad as that old witch-doctor of yours."

Goza made a deprecating gesture, as if to imply that it was not very tactful to dwell on a subject that was better forgotten.

"We had no choice, though our hearts were against it. But that is all past—let the white men now demand of us what they will, for they have freed us from the terror of many years."

Carmichael turned to Half-crown, feeling that he was more likely to understand the workings of the native mind, and how much sincerity there might be in Goza's attitude.

"He ready to lick our boot, baas," Half-crown replied

in his quaint English. " Silly superstition sometimes useful, and keep ign'rant man in proper place. He not dare try any hokey-pokey since you bump off that ol' fraud, for he reckon you big shout now. Oh, yes, baas, you tell 'um and he do it quick! "

Carmichael nodded. He had already formed that opinion but was glad to have confirmation. Once more he addressed Goza, repeating the question he had asked on the previous day about the distance to the nearest white man's town along the coast.

Goza spread out his hands. " Chief, I spoke the truth. I have never heard of the place you name. How should I? None of my people go far from their own villages, nor do any white men come here. Once, many moons ago, two reached the edge of this district, seeking to seize men for labour like the Arab did in the days of my grandfather; but Makubi ordered that they should be driven away and they have not returned."

That therefore was the explanation of the reception the travellers had met with at the first village encountered. Half-crown had been right in his surmise that they had been mistaken for labour agents.

" Very well, then, perhaps you are speaking the truth. But you said you would send for a man who did know. Has he come yet? "

" No, chief. I sent, but he has gone away on a long journey," Goza replied quickly.

" In other words he never existed," came the retort. It was quite true: the headman had invented the man on the spur of the moment, as an added inducement to stay.

Carmichael thought for a minute and decided to tell Goza exactly how matters stood. He spoke of the men who had taken his ship, and of the business they were engaged in.

Goza might not know anything of the coast towns, but rumours had reached him of the past doings of Milverton's liquor-smugglers.

"Ah, chief, I have heard of them. They sell to the young men water that burns the throat like fire and makes them mad. None has come here, for Makubi forbade it and all men feared him; but in other parts there has been much trouble because of it—fights and killings and insolence to headmen. Beer is good and it makes a man happy, but in this burning water lies much evil."

Goza's words confirmed what Carmichael had heard: that the better types of natives were dead against the traffic.

"Those are whom I mean. We are enemies of these men."

"Like the white people in uniform—the police of whom I have heard? I have never seen them, for they are slow and lazy and never come here, although there is a little fort where five of them live not three days' walk from here."

"Ah!" Carmichael exclaimed. "You know the way to this place?"

Goza jerked up his head in the affirmative. "This man here knows. And this." He pointed to a couple of his followers. "They could guide you."

Carmichael turned to Derek. "That's our line, then. Make for this Portuguese police post and set them moving. At the same time we shall find out where we really are. To-morrow at sunrise," he went on to Goza, "we will leave here and travel to this place. Now go, and see that the guides are here and ready to start as soon as the next dawn comes."

CHAPTER TWELVE

WINDING PATHS

THE sun was just about to lift above the horizon next morning when the party pulled out from Goza's village. One of the promised guides marched in front, a couple of spears slanted over his shoulder. Derek and Carmichael followed in his steps along the narrow winding track, while their two henchmen and the second guide brought up the rear.

The existence of a path made travelling a very different matter from what it had been on the journey inland from the coast. Though the forest was still dense in parts, it had been kept cut back along the trail, and formed no obstacle to steady progress. The more difficult stretches were those where the jungle gave place to treeless patches.

Here they encountered the tremendous growth of tropical grass that springs up during the season of the rains wherever it is not stunted by the deep shade of overhanging foliage. As they pushed their way through, drops of water showered down upon them from seed-heads wetted by an overnight storm, while the pencil-thick stems, bent over in places by wind or the passing of big game, tangled their feet and made progress a matter of continual high stepping.

The country through which they were marching was full of wild life, though owing to the thickness of the vegetation very little was visible. Their ears, however, were not so handicapped, and continually they heard large antelopes, wild pigs, and once a herd of buffalo, break away as they were disturbed by the scent and sound of human beings. Unseen flocks of guinea-fowl uttered their clinking note of alarm amidst the undergrowth, monkeys chattered and grimaced in the tree-tops, and brightly coloured finches of many kinds fluttered up from the patches of tall grass as the travellers forced their way through.

Except for a short halt at noon they continued on the move all day, and towards evening reached a fair-sized river, on the nearer bank of which stood a native village. On catching sight of the white men, the inhabitants showed signs of the resentment that had been previously encountered, but a few words from Goza's two guides promptly changed that attitude to one of friendliness. The headman came forward with a present of food, and set his people to clear a patch of ground overlooking the river and erect a rough grass shelter in which Derek and Carmichael could camp for the night.

The two were not sorry to throw themselves down on the bundles of dry grass that had been laid to serve as mattresses, for they were tired after their long day's tramp. Nearby, where their followers were making their camp, the smoke of a cooking-fire was already rising straight and blue into the evening air, and round it several of the local people were gathered, listening eagerly to the tale of recent happenings from the lips of Goza's two men. Cast by the sinking sun, the long shadows of the trees lay athwart them, and behind were the red-brown roofs of the conical huts backed by the deep green of the forest.

Lying on his back, resting his weary legs, Derek slowly turned his eyes from watching the group of natives, and let them rest on the river that ran below the camp.

Already its ripples were tinted with crimson, answering colour for colour with the western sky.

A little way downstream the farther bank was fringed by a shelving sandy beach, upon which lay what looked like several driftwood logs. To Derek's surprise he saw one of these begin to move, and then another: the objects were crocodiles that had been basking there during the daytime heat, and now that the sun was going were returning to the water. Not far from them a couple of herons, heavy after hours of successful fishing in the shallows, took to wing, to be followed by a small mixed flock of egrets and glossy ibis.

Darkness crept up swiftly. The river lost its glow and turned to the colour of lead, and the murk gathered under the bordering trees. V-shaped flocks of wild-duck clove the air as they made for their night-time feeding grounds, and from far up the river came the booming roar of an old bull hippo.

Yoruba, who had taken over the duties of cook, brought the evening meal, which Carmichael and Derek ate with an appetite born of their strenuous day. Pipes were lighted, for they had managed to obtain some native tobacco, and they smoked in silence, each enjoying the contentment of a good feed and peaceful surroundings.

The chatter of their native followers slowly ceased as one by one they dropped off to sleep. Between the huddled forms the fire flickered steadily, its reflection gleaming redly on the overhanging trees and winking a reply to the host of stars above.

With the cessation of nearer sounds the more distant ones became audible. From far away echoed the roar of a lion, while closer at hand were faint rustlings amid the foliage telling of antelopes approaching the river to drink. Somewhere beyond the village a jackal yapped sharply, while from its nest in a hollow tree came the plaintive wail of one of those little marmosets known as bush-babies.

At dawn they prepared to cross the river. Later in the year, when the dry season came, it would be possible to pass over it on foot, but now the water was high owing to the rain still falling up-country. Goza's guides, however, had already made arrangements with the villagers, and a dug-out canoe was ready to ferry the party over.

It was a primitive type of boat, hollowed from the trunk of a single tree, but though it leaked slightly where past suns had cracked its thick sides, it was safer than it looked. Derek and Carmichael embarked first and were paddled across. While the vessel returned to fetch the others they waited beneath a spreading tree from which hung scores of ingeniously constructed nests, the work of a colony of weaver-birds. At last the party reassembled on the farther bank, and the march was resumed.

During the two days' journey Derek and Carmichael learned much of the past doings of the gang who had seized the *Chiwi*, and of the feelings of the better type of native on the whole subject. From various sources they pieced together the methods that had been used for running cargoes.

The smugglers, it appeared, had both white and coloured agents up and down the coast and, having received the tip, the nearest one to the selected spot would make his preparations. The illicit cargo would be brought ashore in boats after nightfall and concealed in different hide-outs in the jungle, from which it would be distributed through secondary agents among the natives.

Knowing the speed with which information will travel from village to village, Derek and Carmichael guessed that the running of a cargo must have been known beforehand. Then they asked why report had not been made to the nearest police post, so that the landing could have been intercepted. The reply was that several times this had been done, but that the Portuguese police were so slow off the mark that they never arrived in the vicinity of the "run" until it was all over.

At last they came in sight of the spot for which they were bound. On the far side of a shallow valley there was a sharp rise of ground, and on its crest stood an irregular group of buildings. These were surrounded by a wall of rough stones, and the encircling trees had been cleared. A sagging telephone wire, supported on bush poles, was strung above the buildings and led away into the forest.

Carmichael and Derek quickened their pace, and reached a little stream that ran down the bottom of the valley. They splashed their way across, but those who followed came to a halt.

"What is it?" Carmichael asked, turning.

The two guides pointed towards the buildings and shook their heads. "We will come no farther, chief."

"Why not?"

They repeated the statement and gave their reason. They had heard many strange tales about the "men in uniform", and preferred not to make contact with them. They said they would rejoin the white chiefs later.

Carmichael nodded, and was about to go on when he noticed that Half-crown also seemed ill at ease. "Are you scared to come up too?" he queried.

Half-crown grinned sheepishly. "If the baas want me I come, but if not want me I stop here and save climb up hill. Never did like police feller—seen too much of um. This place good for camp, baas; when you finish talk you find food ready and blanket laid out."

Carmichael laughed. "Yes, I expect you're still wanted by the police in a good many places from what I know of you! All right, you stop here, and Yoruba had better do so too. Come along," he added to Derek, "the sooner we stir those fellows up and get them busy on their decrepit-looking telephone the better."

Side by side the two ascended the hill, for the path they had been following had now widened out into a comparatively broad track. They reached a gap in the rough encircling wall—it could hardly be called a gateway, for the gate itself had fallen from its hinges and was lying on the ground, a prey to the voracious white ant.

They passed through and found themselves traversing a plot of beaten earth facing an irregular half-circle of buildings constructed of mud-brick and unsquared stone. That on the left was clearly the quarters of the native constables, for several black heads appeared at the doorway and stared at the intruders; while that on the right was obviously the lock-up, from its small barred windows high up in the wall. Facing them was an erection fronted by a thatched veranda, which presumably was the abode of the white police. The two crossed towards it.

"Hallo! Anyone about?" Carmichael called.

There was no answer, so they looked into the nearest room. It seemed to be some kind of an office, for it contained a table littered with papers. Carmichael called again, and in response a loud creaking made itself heard. The figure of a Portuguese sergeant, in a state of considerable undress, heaved itself up from a canvas camp bed, and gave vent to a loud ejaculation of surprise. From an adjoining room several other creaks issued, telling of colleagues also rudely disturbed from their prolonged siesta, and tousled heads protruded themselves from a neighbouring doorway.

CHAPTER THIRTEEN

AN UNEXPECTED RECEPTION

THE sergeant got to his feet, clutching at his trousers which promptly began to slip down over his hips. As he demanded to know who the intruders were and what they wanted he tightened his belt and straightened his crumpled tunic.

In the course of his coasting business Carmichael had acquired a fair working knowledge of the Portuguese language. " We have come to report a crime and get you to take action," he said, and began to give a summary of recent events. At the first mention of the *Chiwi* and the smuggling racket, the sergeant gave vent to a loud " Ha! "

" You come from that ship? " he interrupted. " Then you at least are caught! I know all about you and your friends. Our warship is seeking that vessel along the coast, and very soon she shall be captured too."

Carmichael realised that the sergeant's knowledge was a good deal behind the times. Probably official correspondence reached this lonely post by native carrier only at long intervals, and that the last budget received had been sent off from headquarters prior to the *Chiwi's* capture.

" You're a bit out of date," he replied. " She was taken a couple of months or more ago." Carmichael went on to give a summary of what had happened since then: of the auction of the vessel and his purchase of her for the purposes of legitimate trade.

The sergeant snorted angrily. The last official communication he had received had said nothing about this —therefore he could take no cognisance of it. A likely tale! "If the ship is yours, what are you doing here instead of being aboard her?" he demanded. "You look like a man with money to buy a ship!" he added scornfully, pointing to Carmichael's soiled garments, which bore plentiful traces of the mud of the mangrove swamp and the tears of thorns and branches of the jungle.

"I'm telling you, if you'll listen!"

"I'm listening, so go on," came the disbelieving reply.

Carmichael went on with his tale. As he spoke the other police, whom the coming of the visitors had disturbed, gathered round the doorway while, seeing that something unusual was happening, several of the native constables drifted across from their quarters, trailing rusty rifles to which long bayonets were attached.

At the end of the recital the sergeant gave another disgusted snort.

"A likely tale! Lies from beginning to end! I know you—you're some of those rogues we've been trying to catch!"

Carmichael was beginning to get annoyed. "Rubbish!" he ejaculated. "If we were what you say, do you think we'd be fools enough to come here just for the pleasure of spinning you a yarn?"

The other gave a comprehensive shrug. "No doubt you have some reason for doing so, perhaps to draw us off in one direction while you land a fresh cargo in another. You are English, and you think we Portuguese are fools, eh? But we are not! You have come here, and here you will remain until we find out more about you."

"Do you mean to say you're going to detain us? You've no right—— "

"Right?" the sergeant blazed out. "We've plenty of right! It's you who have none to be in this area! Here you remain until we know much more about you both than we do now."

"If you don't believe what I've told you about the *Chiwi* being sold to me, and who I am, ring up Beira and ask your people there for confirmation. You've got a telephone, for we saw the wire and poles."

"It is out of action. No doubt elephants have pulled down the line. One day it may be repaired, perhaps when the rainy season is over. Meanwhile, here you stop."

Carmichael's consternation showed in his face. If the obstinate sergeant had been a partner of Campbell and his friends he could not have played into their hands more effectually! Even if an inquiry about Carmichael and Derek were sent by the next native messenger carrying routine communications, weeks might elapse before anything was done either about themselves or the stolen ship. The rogues would be able to complete their business undisturbed, sink or otherwise dispose of the *Chiwi*, and safely cover their trail!

The sergeant caught sight of Carmichael's expression and chuckled.

"Aha, *Senhor* Englishman! That upsets whatever scheme you were planning, eh?"

Carmichael's hold on his temper frayed through at last. Turning on the sergeant he gave him a short and pithy account of what he thought of his brain, his appearance, and his future.

The man stepped back before the sudden violence, and snatched up a large revolver that had been lying among the papers on the table. "Seize them and take them off to the lock-up," he shouted to his subordinates at the door.

" Wait," he added as they jumped to obey. " Search them first, and hand over anything you find to me."

The search of Derek and Carmichael did not take long, for their garments were few. The result was only a couple of pipes, a box of matches and some tobacco, and Derek's pistol, at the sight of which the sergeant became even more excited. He seemed to think he had had a narrow escape from it being used on him. In his mind it clinched the conviction that he had made an important capture.

At that lonely post the arrest of white men was an almost unprecedented event, and one which called therefore for some show of ceremony. They must be taken across to the lock-up in style. The sergeant marched in front, Derek's pistol in one hand and his own revolver in the other, while behind him Derek and Carmichael were brought along by his four colleagues. As a rear-guard, came eight or nine native constables in faded uniforms, each carrying a rifle to which a long old-fashioned bayonet seemed permanently fixed.

The lock-up was reached, the two Englishmen thrust inside, and the door firmly fastened behind them.

The cell in which they found themselves contained no furniture beyond a couple of wooden bunks. In size it was about eight feet each way, but its rough stone walls rose up nearly double that measurement, and were broken only by the stout door through which the two had entered, and a small barred window set high up near the ceiling and far out of reach of any occupant.

As the footsteps died away outside Derek and Carmichael looked ruefully at each other.

" Here endeth the first lesson! " Carmichael remarked cynically. " It's a lesson that's taught me something, too, and that is just what a fool I've been! I wish to goodness the idea of roping in the Portuguese police had never occurred to me—if you want anything done in this world you've got to do it yourself."

" Well, we couldn't tell," Derek commented. " And anyway, there didn't seem to be an alternative."

" We ought to have thought of something somehow," Carmichael replied vaguely. " Perhaps enlisted the help of local natives, who seem to be friendly towards us now, and who certainly don't like Campbell and Co. and their doings. If they're running a fresh cargo we might have found out where, and worked out some plan of getting our own back. But as long as we're stuck in this foul hole, the beggars can have it all their own way."

" How long do you think it will be before our identity is established and we're released," Derek asked.

" How should *I* know! " Carmichael responded petulantly. " Months, probably, considering the usual dilatory methods of these fellows, and by that time . . . Oh, curse! We've got to get out somehow, but I'm dashed if I can see how it's going to be done! "

Derek nodded. " The door looks hopeless, but I wonder if anything could be done about that window." He peered upwards at it. " The bars are wood, not iron."

" Huh! How are we going to reach 'em in the first place, and what are we going to cut them with in the second? Even if you stood on my shoulders I doubt if you could touch them with your fingers, and though they may be of wood, they're almost as tough as iron by the look of 'em. We'll have to think of something better than that! "

Conversation languished, for each became busy with his own thoughts. The hours passed. Towards evening the door opened and food was thrust in, together with a couple of blankets. The light from the window above

faded, telling of the coming of night, and presently the
cell became pitch dark. Tired of speculating on what
might have been, or what might still be done if only a
message could be got through to a more responsible
authority, the two captives made themselves as comfortable as they could on the hard wooden bunks and tried
to get some sleep.

Meanwhile, after Derek and Carmichael had started up
the hill, leaving the rest of the party behind them, Half-
crown and Yoruba looked around to choose a suitable
camping-site. They had no desire to go far from the
stream, for that would lengthen the distance that water
would have to be carried; on the other hand they had a
strong preference for somewhere that was not in full view
of the police post, a point with which Goza's two men
heartily agreed. After a little search they chose a spot
not far from the path and water, but well screened by
trees from the buildings that crested the slope.

They had expected Derek and Carmichael to be away
some time, and it was not until towards evening that they
began to wonder why they did not return. It struck them
as odd, knowing that they would not have much in common with the Portuguese police, or be likely to linger
once business discussions had been completed.

Presently a local savage was seen coming down the
slope. He crossed the stream, and, catching sight of the
little camp, halted in surprise, and then turned aside to
speak.

He had come from the post, it appeared, having been
to see a relative who was a native constable there, and he
was full of what he had recently witnessed, as an en-
thralled spectator in the background. With a wealth of
detail he described the lay-out of the buildings, the way
that two white men had, under an escort of bayonets,

been marched across the earthen square to the lock-up, and the speculations that were rife among the native police as to what crime they had been committing.

The news filled Half-crown and Yoruba with consternation. Their first thought was about themselves—would the police come down and arrest them too? Goza's men thought not, for unless the white chiefs had spoken of them, their presence would not be known, and no travellers using the path had passed in that direction. Their minds being relieved about this, they began to consider what next should be done.

Around the little fire they had lighted the four squatted shoulder to shoulder, Half-crown and Yoruba doing most of the talking and Goza's men putting in a word occasionally. The night had fully come before an agreement had been reached.

Worry does not always keep a man awake: sometimes mental exhaustion has the opposite effect. Carmichael dropped off to sleep almost at once, while Derek, who had far less at stake, found it impossible to do so. He lay first on one side and then on the other, but whatever position he tried he was conscious of the hardness of the bunk beneath him and the lack of a pillow under his head.

Time passed for him in restless turning. He heard the chatter of the native constables across the square die away, and presently the voices of the sergeant and his companions from their quarters nearby also ceased. At last Derek felt a welcome drowsiness steal over him, and he dropped off into a fitful slumber.

" Baas! "

The word penetrated into Derek's consciousness as part of a dream in which Half-crown, clad in the uniform of a Portuguese general, was trying to warn him against performing a Highland fling to a tune played by the engines of the *Chiwi*.

"Baas, you in there?"

This time Derek realised that the voice came from outside his dream. He sat up, and at the sound of his movement the question was repeated.

He glanced round and then upwards, towards where the barred window showed as an indigo square against the surrounding darkness. Against the stars behind, a round black object was silhouetted.

"Half-crown! Is that you?" he whispered back.

The head lifted itself a few inches. "Ya, baas, I here," came the eager reply. "Cut long pole in bush and bring it for climb up."

Derek swung his feet to the floor and stood up. On the other side of the room he heard his companion also stir.

"Good man!" Carmichael murmured as he became aware of the situation. "Can you manage to shift those bars and get us out of here?" he asked, looking up at the blob that was Half-crown's head.

"Ya, baas, I cut 'um," came the whispered reply. "Axe no good—police hear chop and wake up—but knife do it though take plenty time."

Clinging to the rough-barked pole that he had brought to serve as a primitive ladder, Half-crown began to whittle at one of the bars with his clasp-knife. From the start it was obvious that he was going to be right about the time question, for the wood was hard and well seasoned and the position in which he had to work was an awkward one. Silence reigned except for the distant calls of wild animals away in the bush and the scraping of the knife, while shavings of wood began to fall in an intermittent shower inside the cell.

Derek measured with his eye the height of the window

above him. "Even if he gets them cut," he murmured to Carmichael, "I don't see how we're going to get up there unless he's brought a rope."

"He's no fool, and will have thought of something," the other replied in the same low tone.

At last the base of one of the bars was severed, and after a short pause to rest his aching hand and wrist Half-crown began on where it entered the stonework at the top. A tug and a light snap and the bar was out. The head vanished for a moment as the severed piece was handed down to an unseen confederate below to be laid silently on the ground, and the work on the next bar commenced.

When the gap was wide enough to wriggle through, Half-crown made a sign to whoever was waiting below, and from the movements of his head and shoulders he seemed to be lifting something heavy. The end of a stout pole appeared at the opening, lengthening and sinking as Half-crown worked it over the sill. Down it came, while those inside lifted their hands to grasp it. With a slight slithering sound and a shower of rasped bark, the butt of the pole was gently lowered to the floor.

Carmichael tied his boots round his neck by the laces, and Derek did the same. First one and then another shinned up the wobbling pole, praying that the butt would not slip, for the crash of its fall would wake everyone within earshot. Negotiating the hole in the window was an acrobatic feat for not only was it a tight squeeze but the ends of the cut bars projected like teeth. However, getting through was safely accomplished, and with considerable relief they slithered down the corresponding pole outside to where Half-crown and one of Goza's men waited at the foot.

Half-crown silently led the way towards the gap in the encircling wall, the two white men following gingerly on unaccustomed bare feet. Once through the gap they paused to replace their boots, and there Goza's men caught them up carrying the pole down which they had slid. There was no sense in leaving it as an obvious clue which would be seen by the first person who woke, while the cut bars and the pole inside the cell might not be noticed until someone entered with breakfast. The longer the prisoners' flight remained undiscovered, the more chance there was of getting well away.

It was now safe to speak, and Carmichael murmured a word of praise and thanks to Half-crown and his companion, and asked about the others.

"Yoruba and savage wait down by stream," was the reply. "Look after stores. Not want 'um come up: two men not make noise but four do. Hurry, baas, not long now before light come."

It was true. Owing to the time taken in cutting through the bars it was nearly dawn. The morning star was already above the horizon. The party hastened forward through the darkness, made contact with the other members, and set to work to cover as great a distance as possible before the escape should be discovered.

The first streaks of grey appeared in the east, making marching considerably easier, for now they could see where to put their feet. By the time the sun rose, the party had put more than a couple of miles between themselves and the police post.

Everything now depended on how much start they could get, for both Derek and Carmichael had little doubt that they would be pursued. With luck, however, some time might elapse before the spoor of their booted feet was discovered, and until then the police would be ignorant of the direction they had taken.

CHAPTER FOURTEEN

LIGHTNING REFUGE

Noon found them still travelling but beginning to feel the effect of their exertions, and Carmichael decided to call a halt.

" I think we can safely take a short rest now," he said to Derek. " We must have covered a dozen miles at least, and we ought to consider where we're going to make for eventually. Besides, I don't know what you think about it, but I'd be glad of something to eat."

" So should I," Derek admitted. " I'd forgotten we'd had no chance of a bite of breakfast, and what they lashed out to us last night wasn't exactly filling."

" We'll turn off the path and find a bit of thick bush. Not that I think they're on our track yet, but it'll be wise to take precautions."

" Considering the pace we've been travelling I shouldn't think there's much fear of anyone catching up with us yet," Derek commented. " From what I saw of that sergeant and his companions they didn't look exactly athletic—in fact I should say that half an hour of tramping would fag them right out."

" Oh, them! " Carmichael replied with a laugh. " I've no fear of those chaps; they're soft and lazy from lying about all day with nothing to do and nobody to keep them up to the collar. They'll leave the job to their native constables, and it's them I'm anxious about, for they're tough and good trackers. They'll be scouring the bush and questioning any local natives they see, and unfortunately we've met one or two on the path this morning, who might talk. Moreover, those native police will be without white supervision, and if some of them came on us they wouldn't think twice about using their rifles and those beastly bayonets they're so fond of! Remember we've nothing to fight back with, not even that pistol of yours now."

The party moved off the track and, having picked a suitable spot, built a small smokeless fire of dry sticks and cooked some food. Just as they had finished eating and were preparing to move on, one of Goza's men emitted a sharp hiss and stood listening.

Derek and Carmichael had heard nothing, but clearly the native had done so. He knelt and laid his ear to the ground; then he rose quickly to his feet, making a sign that was unmistakable.

Half-crown promptly stamped out the remains of the fire with his dilapidated boots, while Yoruba thrust the bundles of stores more deeply out of sight beneath some undergrowth. The whole party lay down and waited tensely.

Through the stems of the sparse grass that grew beneath the trees they caught sight of a couple of uniformed natives hurrying along the path at a jog-trot, each carrying his weapon ready for instant action. Swiftly they passed on, and the pad of their steps died away.

" Quick, they are gone for the moment, but they may return as soon as they see no more spoor on the trail," said the savage who had first given the alarm. " We cannot double back, for there may be others following. We must take to the bush, where they will find it harder to trail us."

In the wake of the guide the party threaded their way through the trees, moving as silently as possible. They had not covered more than half a mile when they heard behind them a peculiar high-pitched call, such as natives use for transmitting news over long distances, and all knew that the men they had seen had realised they had overshot the mark and were casting back. Worse still, from somewhere in front, came like an echo an answering cry. There was a second patrol trying to head them off, and there might be others as well.

The guide turned sharply, taking a new line of retreat, and as he did so he beckoned Half-crown to his side and began to speak rapidly. Half-crown nodded once or twice, grinned at the thoughts that were passing through his brain, and dropped back to where Carmichael and Derek followed to report.

"Baas," he said rapidly, "that native man tell me somefin. Not far up that way"—he pointed in the direction the man was taking—"he say there is a village where no man live, for year ago one of the huts was struck by lightning."

"Well, what of it?" Carmichael asked without slackening his pace, for another long-drawn call in the distance had indicated yet another foraging patrol.

"You forget, baas, these are wild, savage, silly, superstitious beggars. When a village is hit by a flash out of the sky they think it under curse of spirits, and run away quick and build another at new place. He say he know white men not afraid of unseen power, for did they not kill that old fraud Makubi with their magic? Idea of savage very silly but useful sometimes" he continued with a derisive grin. "If we go there, native police not dare follow, he say—they go back to Portuguese and tell them spoor lost and can't find!"

Carmichael remembered having heard before of that theory about lightning which is common all over Africa.

"Good enough," he exclaimed. "The sooner he shows us the place the better!"

"He not go close for he proper scared of it, but he tell us, baas. See, he stop now," Half-crown added, as the figure in front halted.

"The place on which the curse fell is yonder," the native said, pointing. "If the white chiefs go forward they will reach it in the time that it takes a man to eat a bowl of maize-porridge. We two"—he indicated himself and Goza's other guide—"will slip away among the trees and go to that village we passed an hour ago. We will be there when the chiefs need us again, for the men with guns and long knives know us not and do not seek us."

With a quick word of thanks Carmichael and Derek pushed on, but Half-crown could not resist a parting gibe.

"Run quickly, or your spooks will come up and give you a good hard nip behind, and their pinches are worse than sting of scorpion!" As the men vanished he grinned at Yoruba who was keeping pace beside him, and added in Swahili, "It is good that there are fools in this world, so that wise men may make use of them."

"Allah is great. He knew that, so he made both, even as he created the lion to prey on the buck," Yoruba commented sententiously. "Evil djinns there are, but not such as these savages imagine; the only true ones are those of which the Prophet spoke."

Half-crown's only reply was a grunt. Privately he thought that Yoruba was almost as superstitious as the local heathen, for he himself was essentially a hard-boiled materialist.

Meanwhile Derek and Carmichael, pushing on in front, emerged on what had once been the cleared ground surrounding the village. Everywhere the swift-growing tropical foliage had sprung up. Old tree-stumps had sprouted again and tall weeds had taken root, and it was no longer an open space of beaten earth but a breast-high tangle of vegetation. They forced their way through, and reached the huts.

Though not long had passed since the place had been abandoned, many of the primitive dwellings of poles and thatch were already sagging. Some had even collapsed, their foundations having been industriously eaten away by white ants, and the wind and the pluck of swaying creepers had done the rest. In the middle, near the village council-tree that grew strong and green above the ruins, three bare patches of charred wood and rain-washed ash marked the sites of the huts which the lightning had destroyed.

" Cheerful sort of spot! " Derek commented when they had taken a good look round.

" We might go farther and fare worse," was Carmichael's reply. " Those trees are tall and thick," he went on, glancing towards the encircling forest, " and there's no hill from which we can be overlooked. Those police natives may in time come to suspect that we've taken refuge here, but they'll be jolly careful not to come and find out. They're recruited from the surrounding tribes, so you can be sure that they know all about the local taboos."

As a place to make their camp, they chose the ground beneath the spreading tree that dominated the desolate village, and here the axe they possessed came in useful for clearing away the undergrowth and weeds. The foliage above would provide a convenient umbrella of shade but, as Derek pointed out, it would prove a leaky one in the case of rain, and there was still a chance of a few late storms, though the wet season was passing.

Carmichael agreed. Existing huts could hardly be used, even the less dilapidated ones, but there was no reason why some of the material should not be pressed into service for the erection of a rough shelter. Half-crown and Yoruba were set to work on the job of collecting undamaged poles and thatch.

The huts might be deserted by their owners but they were not unoccupied! As soon as pulling-down operations in quest of material began, the present tenants appeared and showed their annoyance at being so rudely disturbed. Snakes slithered out, hissing venomously, making Half-crown jump, and Yoruba lash at them with a long stick. Bats squeaked and fluttered round blindly in the sunlight; lizards scuttled away into the undergrowth; while the number of hopping, flying, and crawling insects that emerged would have gladdened the heart of any enthusiastic " bug-hunter." Those who saw them, however, regarded them with disgust, knocking them from their clothing and muttering angrily when they flew with careless abandon into their faces.

The ruins also supplied thoroughly dry wood, a big point where it was a question of making a small fire for cooking, the smoke of which must not be seen. The only times when it would have to be put out entirely would be around the hours of dawn and sunset, when smoke invariably rises and hangs in trailing blue wisps—a sign of occupation that can be seen for miles.

As the afternoon passed towards evening, Derek and Carmichael began to feel more reassured. They had neither heard nor seen anything of those who were seeking them. Apart from the sinister reputation of the deserted village, it was quite possible that the native police had genuinely lost their trail, for the fugitives had jinked several times while threading the bush, and footmarks

do not show on fallen leaves and grass as they do on a bare
path.

Night came on, and with the fall of darkness the party
became unpleasantly aware that the creatures seen when
the tumbledown huts had been disturbed were not the
only frequenters of the spot. The tangled undergrowth
and rotting thatch harboured myriads of mosquitoes,
which emerged in clouds, eager for blood, while the
glimmer of the firelight attracted, from the same refuge,
a veritable army of scorpions. With poisonous tails uplifted and pincers projecting they advanced with a faint
rustling sound to investigate, and only some strenuous
work with burning brands induced the survivors to
retreat.

The scorpion battalions had not long been defeated
before there was another disturbance, this time from a
couple of lions. They had been in the habit of passing
through each night to drink at what had been the village
waterhole nearby, and they resented the presence of
intruders. Though the great cats made no attack on the
encampment, for more than an hour they roamed round
it, giving vent to low grunts and growls of protest and
keeping the unarmed party awake and anxious. It
brought considerable relief when at last the unwelcome
visitors finally decided to take themselves off.

For two days the party remained at the abandoned
village, undisturbed by human beings but chafing at the
inaction. Had the native police gone, or were they still
prowling about the district? Time was precious, yet
Derek and Carmichael knew it would be folly to emerge
and get themselves shot, or at best recaptured, by making
a move too soon. News they must have, and it must be
sought for—no local man would bring it to them.

It was Derek who suggested a possible course of action.

" Those police natives are after us," he said, " and would be on to us instantly if they saw us, for there are no other white men in the area. But they know nothing about Half-crown and Yoruba, and would not connect them with us. What about sending them to scout, and perhaps get in touch with Goza's two guides, who said they would wait at a certain village? "

When approached, Yoruba did not take at all kindly to the suggestion. Leaving his natural element, the sea, had been bad enough, he felt, but at least he had been under the aegis of two white men. But the idea of undertaking a journey without their protection, even though it might be only nominal, to some community of heathen savages, put the wind up him completely. Hastily he began to make excuses: he was cook and could not be spared—he did not know the local language—nor the country, and he would get lost.

Half-crown, however, did not know the meaning of nerves, and had no misgivings at all. He had been thoroughly bored during the last two days with nothing to do, and he accepted the suggestion eagerly. Picking up the small axe to serve as a weapon if one were needed, he stumped off through the encircling weeds and was soon lost to sight among the trees.

Some three hours later Half-crown returned, more laden than he had started, for, in addition to a bundle of meal and sweet-potatoes, he carried a large pot of native beer. The broad smile on his face showed also that he was carrying a certain amount inside as well, for the local brew had met with his entire approval.

" Fine feller at village, baas," he announced as he came up. " See what they give me without asking! "

" Yes, yes," Carmichael said impatiently. " But what's the news? Are those police still about? "

"Poof! They gone. People at village tell me everything. Police come, say they lost spoor in bush, and start asking questions, but people look silly and say nothin'. They ask Goza's two men, not knowing they were with us when we run from post but they play same game. Then they make headman give them meal, and go back to Portuguese fort to say they can't find."

"Did they suspect that we'd taken refuge here?"

Half-crown grinned. "P'raps they did, but they not say, and village man say nothin' neither. Much bad luck to talk about this place: spirit get ratty and tickle 'um up proper." He chuckled derisively. "All they want is for police to go away and not stay around."

"Then if the coast's clear we'd better get out of this dismal place."

"Ya, baas, and come down to that village I been to," Half-crown replied eagerly. "They think we proper big shout for stopping here and not being scared of lightning curse—Goza's man tell 'um too about the way we handle Makubi. They'll give us anything we ask 'um."

"Always on the make, aren't you?" Carmichael grinned. "I suppose it's more free beer you're after."

Half-crown looked hurt. "No, baas," he said indignantly, "they brew good stuff, but that not what I was thinking. Listen, baas, when I there big headman come, who is chief of all this district. I talk to 'um. I speak about evil white men who take our ship. I tell 'um we want her back. He say he too hate these men plenty. You come and talk to 'um, baas."

"The Portuguese police being worse than useless to us," Derek commented, "if we're to do something on our own it might be well worth interviewing this chap."

"Most certainly it would," Carmichael agreed. "We'll get out of here at once."

CHAPTER FIFTEEN

A TRAP MISFIRES

WHEN Derek and Carmichael reached their destination they found that Quazi, the chief whom they sought, had already left and returned to his own place a dozen miles away. Feeling that it was important to make contact with him, they made their way thither under the guidance of one of the local people.

News of their coming had already flown ahead of them, and on the outskirts of his big village they were met by Quazi himself. He was an elderly native with keen black eyes and surprisingly well-formed hands and feet, and having the dignity and perfect manners that are found among Africans of high rank who have not been spoiled by contact with undesirable types of Europeans.

He greeted Carmichael and Derek with a deference not unmixed with awe, for had they not shown that they were impervious to the unseen influences in which he himself firmly believed. In his mind he considered them of a very different standing from the only other white men he knew about—the Portuguese police whose dilatory ways he despised, and persons like Campbell and his associates. After greeting his visitors he said as much, dwelling especially on the smugglers, of whose activities he strongly disapproved.

" It is of these men we have come to speak to you," Carmichael said.

" So I have been told by the man-from-the-south, your servant," Quazi replied, pointing to Half-crown.

" Then if you know the facts I need not repeat them. Those men have gone, taking my ship, but they will come again bringing more of the burning water that makes those who drink it become mad and unruly, and cause strife in the villages. You want this stopped and I want to regain my ship, and we ask you to give us your help."

" Indeed I will," Quazi replied gravely, fingering the string of leopards' claws that hung about his neck. " The police—you know them!—and as for ourselves we have no means of preventing the evil drink being brought from beyond the Great Water. But if you will tell us what you want us to do, it shall be done."

" I understand that rumours of a landing are generally known before it happens? Find out when the next one is expected, so that we can prepare a plan."

" It shall be done. I will send men at once to the villages near the coast, and any news they may hear they will bring swiftly. Meanwhile let the white chiefs and their followers remain here; my people shall build them a new hut and bring food. I will tell them now, and it shall be ready by sunset." Quazi turned to those behind him, and issued a string of sharp orders that set them running.

When the two were alone again, Derek asked Carmichael what he intended to do when the report of a prospective landing should be received.

" I haven't the faintest notion," was the frank reply. " It will have to depend so much on circumstances. We don't know when they'll come—though obviously it will be soon, for the whole idea was to do the job and disperse before we could reach any civilised spot and put a spoke in their wheel. Above all, we're entirely ignorant as to where—it might be a creek on the coast nearby or a hundred miles away. If it comes to that, we don't even know where we are ourselves, for none of the local natives can tell us the distance to any port I can identify. A tough proposition, I'll admit; but it's not going to stop me trying to get even with the swine!"

In the matter of the hut Quazi was as good as his word, and by sunset a rough but effective building of poles and thatch had been run up. A good supply of native food also was brought, but when it came to supper-time, Carmichael left his plate almost untouched.

"Hallo, what's the matter?" Derek asked. "Aren't you feeling fit?"

Carmichael put his hands to his head. "I'm feeling rotten, and I know the reason. I've a dose of fever coming on. It's not surprising after the way we've been bitten by mosquitoes lately—they must have filled us up with malarial germs. I shall have to go and lie down," he added, rising unsteadily to his feet, his limbs beginning to shake and his teeth to chatter with ague.

It was an anxious night for Derek. The attack was a sharp one, and they possessed nothing in the way of necessary drugs to bring down the temperature and rout the germs working in the blood. By midnight Carmichael was delirious, and Derek, who was unused to the usual course taken by that curse of the African coast, began to fear that his companion would not recover. Towards dawn, however, the delirium passed, and by the following morning Carmichael was through the worst of the bout, although it had left him terribly weak and exhausted.

It was about noon that Quazi received a message relayed by one of the spies he had sent out, and he came across himself to report.

The information was brief but significant. A certain trader who, as Quazi put it, was neither a white man nor a black one, had entered the district. He was journeying in the direction of a certain creek on the coast, although there were no villages near it, and therefore a trader could have no legitimate reason for going there. Quazi also declared that this man had been connected with a previous " run " of smuggled liquor.

" Looks pretty certain that the fellow is one of their agents," Carmichael murmured when he heard. " Going to have a look round and make arrangements about hiding and distributing the stuff when it comes ashore. Where does Quazi say the place is? Twenty miles from here? Good thing it's not two hundred, as it might well be. But we've got to find out a lot more before we can work out any scheme. Oh, lor'! I wish I didn't feel such a wreck! This infernal fever's done me, and I shan't be able to do much for at least another couple of days. You'll have to go there by yourself and find out more details somehow. Take Half-crown with you—he's got his head screwed on the right way and should be helpful."

" But what about you? " Derek protested. " I don't like the idea of going off while you're still sick."

" Don't worry about me—I'll be okay. Yoruba'll attend to my wants, and I'm through the worst. Get along as quick as you can, make contact with Quazi's spy, and use his relay system to transmit any messages. I'll follow you in a day or two, and if you get hold of any-thing urgent I'll be along at once, even if I have to get Quazi's people to carry me in a m'shiela slung on a pole! "

" All right, I'll be off, then," Derek agreed, for Car-michael was certainly much better and it seemed safe to leave him. Yoruba was devoted to him, and Quazi could be trusted to send for anything that was needed.

Though there was no possibility of covering the twenty

miles before sunset, Derek made a start at once, for at least he could cover part of the way before nightfall. A little party of Quazi's young men, armed with spears and light axes, led the way, and behind Derek tramped Half-crown, grinning at the prospect of a possible scrap with someone before many hours had passed.

That night they spent beside a lonely waterhole in the middle of a stretch of jungle which teemed with wild life. The men who formed the escort had made up a couple of huge fires of deadwood on either side of the camp, but even then Derek, who had not yet acquired the indifference to such things that long experience of them can bring, felt decidedly nervous at times.

Again and again a sharp crack like a rifle-shot echoed through the dark forest, telling of elephants breaking down branches as they fed. A little more than a hundred yards away a lion, having pulled down some unfortunate beast, made the air quiver with roar after roar as he called up his mate to share his feast. Once a herd of buffalo came straight towards the camp, intending to drink at the waterhole, and only the bright flicker of the flames made them turn aside from their course; while shortly before dawn an impala antelope bounded into the circle of light and out of it again, closely pursued by a pack of ravenous wild dogs, whose long, mottled bodies and lolling tongues shone redly from the glow of the fires. For Derek it was a night of much disturbance, and he was not sorry to see the sky lighten once more in the east.

At length Derek and those with him reached the village that was their objective, and where they were to meet the man who had sent the message to his chief. On arrival they found that he was not there and, not knowing where he might be, they had to await his return.

An hour later he appeared and, seeing Derek, came

forward and saluted. His latest report was not very satisfactory. Possibly the trader had realised that an undue interest was being taken in his movements; he had diverged abruptly from the course he had been following, and had taken to the bush—a move which had effectually shaken off surveillance. The native now frankly admitted that he did not know where " Zeffon "—as he called the trader—was making for. He would return and try again, he said, as soon as he had had something to eat.

He joined a group of local people who were gathered round a communal cooking-pot, eating the stiff porridge it contained with their fingers. A few minutes later a fresh figure appeared on the scene—a stranger passing through on a journey, as the bundle he carried indicated.

The fellow paused near the group and eyed the pot hungrily. A greeting was exchanged and an invitation issued. With alacrity the man put down his bundle and joined in the meal.

As natives will, he chattered of what he had seen on his journey that morning, and presently he mentioned casually that he had seen " Zeffon," expressing surprise that he was in those parts. Immediately Quazi's man began to sit up and take notice, and extracted more details, while the escort that had come with Derek and Half-crown drifted nearer, as if by chance.

They let the stranger finish his food, and then informed him that he would be impounded as a guide.

The man looked slightly alarmed, but submitted with a good grace. After all, he said, to-morrow was as good as to-day, and he was in no great hurry to reach his intended destination.

In the wake of the guide who had been so brusquely commandeered, Derek and Half-crown set off, accompanied by Quazi's young men. Derek had not yet formed

any plan of what to do if this unknown trader were over-
taken, but at least he hoped to learn more about him than
he knew at present, and any action was better than doing
nothing.

The spot where Zeffon had been encountered was
reached, and the native turned off in the direction of the
sea which lay about four miles away. Almost at once
progress became more difficult, for they were entering
the belt of dense jungle that lay along the coast. The
guide kept steadily on, assuring those who followed that
he was certain where the trader had gone, and that he was
leading them straight to the spot.

An hour passed, and still the party plodded onwards.
The rank smell of mud and rotting vegetation came to
their nostrils, and sullen gleams of foul water began to be
seen here and there between the trees, which were rapidly
giving place to the grotesque mangrove. The guide was
now moving more cautiously, picking his way along
firmer ridges of ground that twisted in and out of the
evil-smelling mud, and repeating to those behind him
that they were nearly through the worst.

Meanwhile Quazi's men had begun to murmur and
look ill at ease. The tangled maze of mud and mangroves
in which they found themselves alarmed them, for it was
very different from the firm ground and forest of their
inland home. Derek also began to feel uncomfortable
about the situation, and presently Half-crown, who was
close behind him, voiced his suspicions.

" Baas, you know what I think? "

Derek turned his head. " What? "

" This put-up job. No creek here where our ship could
come, nor place where rogue feller reckon to meet her.
I tell you what I think, baas; that gay dog in front, he
paid to bring us here and then run and leave us, hoping

we wander round, stick in mud, and never find way out again."

Derek gave an exclamation. The same thought had been vaguely entering his own mind, and now he felt certain that what Half-crown suggested was true! The role of a passing traveller was a pose, and the whole thing had been deliberately planned! He called a halt, and to the relief of those from Quazi's inland village, abruptly ordered the guide to lead them out again.

The man made a gesture implying that all white men were mad, for sane people did not suddenly change their minds like that. With a shrug of his shoulders he turned to retrace his steps. No sooner had he passed where Derek stood than he took to his heels and raced off along the intricate backward trail which he alone knew.

He had reckoned without Quazi's young men, however. Instantly they realised the situation, and three of the swiftest bounded in pursuit. Before the treacherous guide had secured any real start they had caught up with him. The next instant he was flung to the ground, while a spear at his throat warned him that he had better keep still.

Derek gave a sigh of relief, knowing that had the man got away the result might have been grim. " Keep a tight watch on him," he ordered, " and tell him if he tries any more tricks he'll be for it."

Quazi's people pulled the frightened native to his feet and made him go ahead, a spear-point close to his back, meanwhile telling him in lurid phrases what might be done to him in the near future. Twisting and turning, the party at last left the swamp behind, and were once more travelling on the firmer ground beneath the trees.

Presently, at a word from Derek, they halted, for it had occurred to him that further use might be made of

the false guide, their prisoner. With Half-crown's help
he began to question the fellow about his employer.

At first the captive remained stubbornly silent, but
Derek's promise that he should not be harmed if he
answered had the desired effect. In a trembling voice he
began to speak.

He was "Zeffon's" servant, he admitted, adding that
his master knew that an interest was being taken in his
movements. That morning he had received orders to go
to the village in the guise of a travelling native, and if a
white man were there and questioned him, he was
reluctantly to offer his services as a guide. He was then
to lead him into that swamp, by a way his master had
previously shown him, and lose him there.

Derek nodded to himself. It did not greatly surprise
him to hear that a good deal about his intentions and
movements were known to the captive's master. Nothing
remains a secret long in Africa, and the wilder the country
the faster information seems to percolate. The people at
Quazi's village knew, and natives cannot refrain from
chattering round their cooking-fires. Men journeying
through would pick up the tale and discuss it when they
reached their various destinations, for the doings of
strange white men are topics of absorbing interest to
natives. Considering the job on which he was engaged,
"Zeffon" would naturally be alert for any reports affect-
ing him, and it would be little time before it would
reach his ears through the local men in his employ.

Derek demanded to know where the prisoner's master
was now. The man declared earnestly that he did not
know, that having obeyed his instructions he was to go
back whence he came and await his master's return.

Derek had a feeling that the man was probably speaking
the truth. Considering the work in which Milverton's

unknown agent was engaged, he would naturally give away as little as possible for fear of some careless word betraying him. Derek therefore signed to the guards to carry on and take the prisoner back to the village, for obviously he could not yet be released lest he should contact his employer and tell him of the failure of the plan to remove all chance of interference.

At Derek's order the face of the false guide went grey. He had counted on being released immediately. But there was still a chance, for his guards had relaxed their grip while Derek was talking to him. With a sudden twist and a bound he darted off, diving for a thick reed-bed close by that bordered a sluggish stream. He knew well enough where his employer was, and in the reeds he felt confident of dodging his pursuers and carrying word of the failure of the ruse.

With angry shouts and waving spears Quazi's men plunged into the reeds after him. The fugitive doubled, but those behind anticipated the move and had spread out, thrusting their way through the ten-foot stems. Slowly they forced him towards the river, which they felt, would bar his escape.

Realising that he was trapped, the man plunged into the water and began to wade across almost at the same moment as the pursuers emerged on the brink.

Quazi's men pulled up instantly, watching with fascinated eyes and making no attempt to follow. Already the man was half-way across. Then came what those who watched had been expecting. There was a sudden heave and swirl in the water. The fugitive threw up his hands, gave one despairing cry, and vanished from sight.

"Like a lot of nasty things, baas, crocodile very useful sometimes!" Half-crown commented as he returned to report to Derek of the outcome of the chase.

CHAPTER SIXTEEN

FIRE HAS ITS USES

WHEN Derek had left Carmichael and journeyed coast-
wards he had no definite plan in his head, but by the time
he got back to the guide's village one had begun to take
shape. The primary need was to obtain exact information,
and this man whom the natives called Zeffon was the
only likely source. The incident of the false guide and the
swamp showed not only that the fellow was indeed
connected with the *Chiwi* affair, but also that he meant
business. There need be no scruples, therefore, about any
counter-measures taken.

The first consideration was to find out where the man
had gone. According to the original message which had
brought Derek down to the coast, a deep-water creek
existed somewhere in the vicinity, and it was more than
likely, therefore, that the man would be somewhere near
it. The following morning Derek called up Quazi's spy,
ascertained that he knew where the creek lay, and dispatched him to investigate. Meanwhile he himself,
together with Half-crown and the young men who had
accompanied them, remained at the village ready to act
at once upon any report received.

The native struck out through the forest on his quest,
eager to make good his earlier mistake in losing Zeffon's
trail and regain his reputation as a good tracker in the
eyes of the white man and of his overlord Quazi. The
distance was about seven miles and he did not take long

to cover it, moving with a quick yet silent step in and out of the serried ranks of trees.

He reached the creek and worked carefully round its brink, taking care to move in cover and examine each yard of the soft ground for any fresh footmarks. His search was barren, however, for there was no sign of any man, booted white or bare-footed black, having visited the spot.

It was disappointing, but he did not intend to give up. If the foreshore had no message, there might be one awaiting him amid the thick bordering forest. Steadily he cast backwards and forwards, widening his area of search, until he was half a mile from the creek itself, but still without result. Noon passed, but he had no thought of food or rest—he had a reputation that must be re-gained.

Suddenly the native paused. He had encountered what looked like a disused game-path running down in the direction of the creek, yet he knew well enough that it could not be what it appeared, for no animals drink salt water. It must have been beaten by human feet. But the trail was old and partly overgrown, and therefore of no present importance. He was about to pass on when, a little way along it, a broken twig caught his eye. He turned to investigate, and on a bit of soft soil nearby he saw the fresh print of a booted foot.

Instantly the native's whole figure became alert. He turned along the track, following it inland and away from the creek, and bending carefully under any obstruct-ing branch lest the rustle of his movements should betray him. He covered a couple of hundred yards, and saw before him a little clearing in the dense jungle. In the middle of it stood a square building of poles and thatch. No new erection, this, for it was weathered and creepers had crept up it, but equally it was no native hut, for not only are these round and small, but who would choose such a spot?

The native slipped a yard or two nearer, and peered over the cover of some foliage. Through the open door he caught a glimpse of something moving inside, and then a figure came fully into view. The watcher ducked down and crawled away in the undergrowth. As soon as he considered it was safe he rose once more to his feet and started back to the village at a steady jog-trot.

Derek received the news with an exclamation of satisfaction. Now at last he could be up and doing after those long hours of waiting! Clearly that creek had been used before, and the building which the native had described as hidden in the forest no doubt dated from a previous "run," and had served to warehouse a cargo till distributed.

Derek glanced at the westering sun. The place, he understood, was two hours distant in time from the village, and even if a start were made at once there was little chance of reaching it before nightfall. But that, he reflected, might be an advantage—the smugglers' agent was not likely to be absent then, and the darkness would help to hide their approach. Nor would it be wholly black for the return journey, for the young moon was in its first quarter.

Derek rose to his feet, and immediately Half-crown was at his side, a grin on his face and his beloved axe in his hand. Quazi's men also sprang up in readiness and approached.

In a few sentences Derek explained what he wanted, and having made sure that all understood, he signed to the discoverer of the hidden retreat to lead the way.

At a rapid pace they traversed the forest, while the sun

sank lower. Presently it vanished below the horizon, and the dusk gathered beneath the trees. Unseen creatures began to rustle away into the undergrowth before the advancing steps, and the calls of night prowlers to sound among the shrouded glades.

A warning whisper from the guide indicated that they were getting near, and the pace became slower and more cautious. Derek guessed that the man was probably armed, and if he were to be seized without doing any damage surprise was essential. As the edge of the clearing was neared, Derek's followers spread out so as partially to encircle it.

Had their quarry been inside the building the surprise might have been complete, but instead he was cooking some food over a small fire in the open. Moreover he was very much on the alert, for the non-return of his servant on the previous evening had made him suspicious that some hitch had occurred in his plan. Half-crown, who had not the local savages' aptitude for silent movement, trod on a dry stick. Instantly the fellow swung round and tugged a large revolver from his belt. In the faint moonlight he caught a glimpse of moving shadows, and fired.

The bullet whipped past Half-crown's head, making him drop into the undergrowth with a muffled " Ow! " At the sound of a human voice the revolver spoke twice in rapid succession, forcing the others to follow his example and take cover.

Quazi's men were all for making a rush with their spears in the good old-fashioned way. But Derek's orders had been strict, and to disobey him might mean trouble later from their chief. They contented themselves by wriggling a few inches forward, while the moonlight glinted on their polished blades.

The man near the fire caught sight of those gleams, and remembered the skill and accuracy with which such weapons can be thrown. Standing in the open he knew he presented an excellent target, while inside the building he could effectually shoot from cover. Turning, he leaped for the door, and in reply to a quick forward movement on the part of those shadowy figures, he let drive with a couple more shots.

Derek began to feel anxious. He had counted on doing the job without bloodshed, but it did not look as if that were now possible. The fellow seemed to have plenty of ammunition, and a rush on the position would mean several casualties.

For a minute he crouched in the bushes, studying the situation, while Quazi's men lay in the surrounding undergrowth, eagerly awaiting the word. There was a movement beside him; turning his head, Derek saw that it was Half-crown.

"Baas, I get 'um," he whispered. "You let me try."

Derek grunted. "Want to get shot?"

"No fear, baas, but I shift 'um. Listen what I say."

Derek did so, and nodded agreement. There was a slight rustling as the spearmen spread themselves out wider, and then Half-crown emerged cautiously from cover and wriggled towards the windowless wall that formed the back of the building.

Unseen by the man who was keeping up a desultory fire from the doorway, the Cape-boy reached the shadow of the eaves and rose to his feet. There was the splutter of a match, and the next moment he was legging it back for the cover of the sheltering trees.

The thatch was old and dry, and almost instantly the flames spread and burgeoned. With a roar they leaped upwards in vivid tongues of orange and scarlet, topped by whirling sparks and a black plume of smoke; while every branch and leaf of the surrounding jungle became etched in red against the night sky behind.

A figure sprang out of the door of the blazing building and glared round with uplifted weapon. Not a sign could he see of the aggressors, for each one had effectively concealed himself in the undergrowth. For a moment the man stood hesitating, then, as the roof collapsed behind him with a tremendous gush of flames and sparks, he swung round and made for the protection of the forest. As he ran he fired shot after shot into the trees ahead for the benefit of anyone who might be lurking there.

He plunged into the shadows, and the next moment his legs were struck from under him. He came down with a crash, his revolver flying from his hand, and before he could even attempt to rise, a triumphant black body landed on his back. Cursing, he tried to throw it off, but an instant later he was in the grip of half a dozen hands. They pulled him to his feet and held him tight.

" Well done, you've got him! " Derek ejaculated as he came up. " Bring him back into the open, and let's have a look at him."

The men did so. The light of the burning building fell full on the captive's face, and Derek saw that this was no half-breed as Quazi's description had led him to expect by his phrase " neither a black man nor a white one." The man was certainly dark, but there was nothing negroid about him, and by the general look of him Derek put him down as some sort of Levantine.

" Your name is Zeffon, I understand? " Derek began.

The other tossed his head, throwing back his raven locks and projecting an unshaven chin.

" Pah! What name is that? " he replied in English. " My name is Xenophon—Demitrius Xenophon. I am a

Greek gentleman born of Syrian parents in Egypt and educated at best school in Turkey where—— "

" Cut that out—I don't want your life-history, you— you patchwork quilt! " Derek retorted, hardly able to refrain from smiling at the varied catalogue. " It's not your past I want to hear about, but you're present doings."

" What have they got to do with you? " Xenophon snarled back. " You keep your finger outa my pie—you not police! "

" I should have thought you knew very well what business it is of mine, or you wouldn't have made that attempt of yesterday. Which, by the way, came hard on your boy, for a crocodile got him. However, I'm not going to stand here arguing. We'll get back to the village where I'm camped, and go further into the matter there. I expect you've had your supper, but I shall want mine after covering fourteen miles here and back. Besides, that little fire's dying out "—Derek nodded towards the glowing remains of the burned building—" the dew's falling, and the mosquitoes are beginning to bite. So we'll be marching."

" I not stir! " Xenophon retorted violently. " You not police, you no right to arrest me! "

Derek laughed. " Funny to hear you talking about legal rights! You should know well enough there isn't enough law skating about here to fill an empty cartridge-case! "

He signed to the men who held the prisoner, and they began to propel him forward. Xenophon promptly let his legs go limp, and sagged in their hold like a half-filled sack, refusing to move a step of his own will.

The natives at once suggested that a judicious pricking with their spear-points might work wonders, but Derek shook his head. " No, I don't want him damaged in any

way—yet," he replied, stressing the last word significantly. " Now then, Xenophon," he went on, " are you
going to walk as you're told? "

" No! " came the snarling reply.

" All right, then. You'll be carried."

" Like pig on pole, baas? " Half-crown put in with a
chuckle of delight.

" Yes! " Derek retorted. " If he won't walk he can't
complain of a bit of discomfort. Certainly I'm not going
to provide him with a nice hammock, even if I had one,
which I haven't. Go off into the bush and get busy with
that axe you're so fond of."

A long pole was cut, and the grinning natives lashed
Xenophon to it lengthwise with strands of creeper pulled
from the surrounding trees. A couple of bearers heaved
him up, and with the ends of the pole across their shoulders,
started for home at a jog-trot. The others followed,
laughing and chattering as natives do when, in a similar
fashion, they bring in an antelope or wild pig that they
have hunted and killed.

Derek turned and tramped after them, thinking that
the captive must be finding it a most unpleasant way of
travelling, but he had only his own obstinacy to thank
for it. The rear of the party was brought up by Half-
crown, carrying with him the heavy revolver which he
had searched for and retrieved from the undergrowth
where it had fallen from the trader's hand.

CHAPTER SEVENTEEN

THE CAPTIVE SPEAKS

DEREK was more than a little weary when he reached the village. Owing to the darkness, only faintly illumined by the quarter moon, it had proved a far tougher proposition traversing the jungle than the outward journey had been. But late though it was, he must complete the evening's work and extract the enemy's plans from Xenophon before thinking of sleep. It was essential that a message should be dispatched to Carmichael the first thing in the morning, letting him know what time remained in hand before the *Chiwi* was due.

Derek fully expected that extracting information was not going to be easy, for Xenophon had already shown himself to be as obstinate as a mule. However Derek meant to have it, and he thought he saw his way of getting it. Though he had no intention of going to extremes, the prisoner need not know that, and he hoped to be able to scare him into speaking before things started to go too far.

Having gulped down some food Derek crossed to where the captive, now released from his bonds and pole, was sitting sulkily on the ground under the watchful eyes of those who had carried him thither.

" Well now, Xenophon. When are you expecting your friends to arrive in the creek with the cargo? "

" I shall not tell, no! "

" You said something like that before over the question of walking, but the result was the same, though you did the journey far less comfortably. So you'd better think again."

"I shall not tell," came the repetition.

Grins of anticipation spread over the faces of the attendant natives. Though they had not understood the words they guessed their meaning. They had no special animosity against the Levantine trader, indeed they knew very little of him, for he came from another district, but they hoped that his obstinacy was going to provide them with a spot of entertainment.

"Listen to me," Derek went on patiently. "I want certain information, and I'm going to have it."

"Never! You could tie me up and carry me, but you not able to make me speak!"

"Oh, aren't I?" Derek's eyes roved significantly to the nearest cooking-fire and then to the blade of a spear that lay beside it.

One of the spectators intercepted the look, and gleefully picked up the blade and thrust it into the heart of the flames.

"Do you want me to hand you over to these chaps? They'd get a lot of kick out of tickling you up with that red-hot blade. I give you five minutes to make up your mind."

No answer.

Derek waited five minutes, and then shrugged his shoulders. "Hold him down, then."

Instantly Quazi's men had the captive spreadeagled on his back. There was going to be some fun after all! The native who had thrust the spear-head into the fire withdrew it, tapped the white ash from the glowing metal, and flourished it in the prostrate man's face. "Where shall I try first, chief?" he asked eagerly. "Under his armpit or against the inside of his thigh?"

The sweat of fear appeared on Xenophon's dusky forehead. " I will speak, curse you! " he said.

Derek breathed an inward sigh of thankfulness. Things had gone as far as he meant to allow them, and had the man still held out he would have been defeated. " Let him up," he ordered. " Keep that blade handy, though, in case I want it again."

With disappointment on their faces the men obeyed. " Now," Derek went on to Xenophon, " what's the answer to the first question I asked? "

" The day after to-morrow," came the reply. " Two hours after sun has set."

" I presume they wouldn't come in unless they got the okay from you that the Portuguese police weren't about? What is the signal you were to give? "

Silence.

" Where's that spear-blade! "

" No, no. I will tell! " came hastily from the smugglers' agent. " I was to light a fire at the northern end of the creek entrance, where it could be seen from the sea."

" More juggling with lights," Derek commented under his breath, remembering the taking of the *Chiwi*. " Any others to be lit? " he asked aloud.

" At the point where the cargo is to be landed," Xenophon admitted. " Where old path from the building you burn run down to the water."

" And you would be waiting beside it to receive the stuff? "

" Yes, I wait there."

" Who would carry the consignment up from the foreshore? "

" I should have four-five natives to do that."

" Where are they now? Not come yet? "

" No. Come to-morrow."

" I see. I shall take steps to gather them in when they arrive. Now what's the procedure? The *Chiwi* comes in, anchors, and the boats put off with the cargo which they hand over to you? "

" Yes, they hand it over," was the non-committal reply.

" In exchange for cash on the nail, I suppose? " Derek said shrewdly. He guessed that there would be no credit about the business, and that Campbell and his pals would want payment before they let the goods out of their keeping. " Where's the money in question?—you haven't got it on you."

" No, it lie in that hut which you burn like a fool. All gone to ashes. Much money—all my savings! "

Derek laughed pleasantly. " You called me a fool just now, but I'm not such a big one as to believe that. You wouldn't have forgotten to snatch it up before you bolted out into the open. You'd have stopped till the roof fell rather than leave without it. You'd better think up a better yarn than that."

" It where you shall never find it, never! " Xenophon declared excitedly. " It is my money, mine, and you shall not steal it! "

" All right! No need to fly off the handle. I'm not a common thief. It's confidences I want, not cash. I suppose you've buried it somewhere safe in a tin box so that the white ants shouldn't eat the notes, until the moment arrived when you needed it. When all this is over you can go and retrieve it—it's nothing to do with me."

For the first time a look of relief passed across the captive's face. " Ah! You English gentleman, and they do not steal a poor man's savings. I am grateful that you do not force me to say where my money is hidden, so I tell you something you have not ask. When that ship comes the big boss will be on her. So be careful with what you do, for if he catch you he cut your throat quick."

" What—Milverton? "

Xenophon gave an affirmative grunt.

" But Milverton's in Zanzibar," Derek pointed out, " so how can he possibly have got aboard the *Chiwi*? " He knew nothing of the visit which Milverton had paid to the shipping offices of the French-owned line, whose vessels call *en route* to Madagascar, about the time when the *Chiwi* sailed from the island.

The captive gave a comprehensive shrug. " All I know is that he will be aboard. Last time there was muddle made and the ship caught by the police ship; this time he come himself to make sure everything goes right."

This was an unexpected piece of news, and Derek felt that it would need digesting. He put it aside for the present, and made a comment that had been in his mind for some time.

" You people seem to have planned everything out to the last detail," he said. " I can't think how you managed it. I suppose you got your instructions from Campbell, yet he's been at sea since the *Chiwi* was captured."

Xenophon allowed himself to grin. " It was all arrange before that ship of yours arrive off coast," he replied. " Campbell he get cable from Milverton, and he send message on to me. He say he going to get ship, and that I to be here on the day he tell me—the one after to-morrow. I to make lights and get natives for carrying up to the store-hut we built, in the same way we did when we use it before. So I come. As I say—all planned before you know anything about it," he added with pardonable pride.

" The deuce it was! " Derek ejaculated. " Well, your

schemes may have gone without a hitch so far, but they won't end without one if I can help it."

There seemed to be nothing more of importance to be got out of the prisoner and, as it was already after midnight, Derek felt that it was about time to think of getting some sleep. He gave some directions about the guarding of Xenophon, who obviously could not be released until after the *Chiwi* had come. At the first light a runner should go to Carmichael bearing the gist of what he had discovered, and as soon as his employer arrived the whole thing could be discussed and some plan devised to give those who had seized the vessel an unexpected reception.

The swiftly relayed message reached Carmichael within three hours, and the following evening he arrived at Derek's village, looking somewhat haggard after his bout of fever but walking fairly briskly. With him were several natives, led by Quazi the chief who had decided to come himself. Now that he had the backing of two white men who had, in his mind, already shown their strength of will, he intended to be in at the finish in person.

Derek greeted Carmichael joyfully, glad to find him on his feet once more.

" Oh, I'm about fit again," was the reply. " I'll admit though I haven't walked all the way—Quazi and Yoruba insisted on having me carried the better part of it! But I tramped the last part and feel the better for stretching my legs. Well, you seem to have done some good work since you've been here. Let's make ourselves comfortable and then you can give me the details."

Derek did so, recounting in full his recent adventures and discoveries.

" Do you think this man Xenophon is telling the truth? " Carmichael asked when he had finished.

" Yes, I do. I put the wind up him thoroughly. Knowing he is in our power, he'd be afraid of the result if it proved that he had been lying."

" You've got him here safely? "

Derek nodded towards several natives who were standing on guard round some huts. " Naturally," he replied. " And to-day I gathered in his five native allies he was expecting—a lot o' dirty dogs, too, by the look of them. Scooping them in was ridiculously easy; they rolled up here to ask the way to the rendezvous, and much to their surprise found themselves in custody. So the decks are clear, so to speak, for the next move."

" We've got till to-morrow evening, you say? "

" Yes, according to Xenophon. The *Chiwi's* due two hours after sunset."

" That gives us the daylight hours to have a look at the ground and make arrangements. I've formed an idea or two, and I expect you have as well, so between us we should be able to evolve a plan of campaign." Carmichael paused, and then added tentatively, " I wonder if Milverton is really coming, too, as our Levantine friend seems to think. It's possible, for if he'd been quick he'd have had time to meet the *Chiwi* at her loading port. It'll be a slice of luck if he's aboard, for I'd like more than anything to settle that beggar's hash! " he ended with a short laugh.

Far into the night they discussed ways and means, and in the morning Quazi was called into conference about the part he and his retainers were to play. The chief was quick to grasp the points of the scheme, and made several useful suggestions. The only snag was the want of a canoe, which was essential to the working of the plan; but one of the villagers volunteered the information that there was one on the small river where the crocodile had seized Xenophon's servant. Quazi said he would send a party of his men to carry the heavy dug-out through the jungle to the shore of the creek.

Meanwhile Derek and Carmichael went to examine the scene of action. From the vicinity of the burned building they took the track leading down to the water. They surveyed the place where the cargo would be landed, and its surroundings, and they fixed the probable position where the *Chiwi* would come to anchor. When they finally retraced their steps they felt satisfied with their morning's work.

In good time before sunset those who were to take part in the plan were assembled, and final directions were given. A native was dispatched to attend to the matter of the signal fire at the seaward entrance of the creek. Five of Quazi's men, chosen to represent Xenophon's party of workers, took up their station at the point where the boats were expected to land the cargo, while their chief ensconced himself among the nearby bushes, feeling his watchful eye would keep them up to the mark. This done, the two white men, followed by Half-crown and Yoruba, moved away a couple of hundred yards along the edge of the water, to where a couple of local paddlers waited by the canoe which had been laboriously brought overland and hidden among the roots of a small but convenient patch of mangroves.

The sun sank, and the surface of the water took on a leaden tint, while the vivid green of the foliage beyond turned to a black frieze against the darkening sky. Overhead the quarter moon shone down from amid its backcloth of stars, and insects began to shrill and pipe in the surrounding undergrowth.

The creek curved, so that from where Derek and his companions waited the open sea was not visible. The first intimation they would have of the *Chiwi's* arrival would be when she was inside the entrance. Though he knew well that at least a couple of hours must elapse before she was likely to come, Derek could not help glancing continually in the direction in which she would appear, and he noticed that Carmichael also had begun to do the same.

" I hope we're not here on a fool's errand," the latter murmured presently, " and that she will turn up as expected."

" If she doesn't we'll have a word to say to Master Xenophon," Derek replied. " But I think he's told us the truth as far as he knows it."

" Probably," Carmichael agreed. " After all we've told him that we've arranged with Quazi for his men to release him as soon as the job's done, so it would be in his own interest not to lie, otherwise he might be in for some unpleasant minutes. But of course the vessel might be delayed for some entirely unexpected reason," he added, moving a cramped leg to an easier position.

Never had the passage of time seemed so long to Derek. Every minute dragged by on weighted feet, and Carmichael also began to feel the strain of expectancy. Behind them they could hear Half-crown fidgeting impatiently, and only Yoruba remained calm and stoical—an attitude that was shared by the two canoe-men, to whom both time and surroundings were a matter of no account.

It was Half-crown who first caught the sound, and gave a warning hiss. A few moments later all had heard it—the throb and wash of a ship's propeller. Every eye turned towards where she would appear, and presently a dark mass loomed up as it slowly rounded the curve. The vessel came nearer, moving ghost-like over the dark water and burning no lights, but as the moonlight picked out her shape more clearly there could be no doubt about her being the *Chiwi*.

She drew onwards, eagerly watched by those who waited in the shadows, and even Yoruba lost his attitude of indifference at the sight of " his " ship. The ting of the bridge telegraph reached their ears, and the water ceased to boil under the counter. With a rattle of chain-links the anchor went down, and the *Chiwi* came to rest almost at the exact spot previously estimated by Carmichael.

Now that she was invisible from the sea and surrounded by the tall jungle bordering the creek, lights began to appear on the vessel's deck, and moving figures to become visible. There was a creak of ropes and sheaves as a boat was lowered into the water, and a tapping of mallets as wedges were knocked out and a hatch-cover removed. More lights appeared, and against them was silhouetted the busy forms of the native crew carrying cases on their heads, lowering them into the boat, and running back for more.

Deeper and deeper the boat sank in the water under the load that was being piled amidships, until at last only a few inches of freeboard were left—and the boat held as much as she could carry. Two figures then scrambled down into the boat, one taking her tiller in the stern and the other getting to work with a pair of oars at her bow. The watchers guessed that the man aft was either Gould or Campbell, while the rower was clearly one of the native crew.

Gingerly the boat was pulled across the placid water towards the spot where the fire gleamed ashore and Quazi's people waited patiently beside it. Meanwhile the second boat was lowered from the steamer, and those aboard began to fill her also with more of the smuggled consignment.

CHAPTER EIGHTEEN

THE BATTLE OF THE BOATS

As the boat approached, the natives who had been squatting round the fire near the water's edge rose to their feet, stretching and yawning. They had been coached in the parts they were to play and were well aware that, from the screen of foliage behind, their chief's eyes were upon them. As the laden craft touched the bank they moved forward together and began to unload her as if they were performing a familiar act, dumping the cases on the ground beside the fire.

Gould, for it was he who had been holding the tiller, stepped ashore and looked round for the agent whom he was to meet. Not seeing him, he turned to one of the busy natives and asked a question.

The man addressed paused for a moment to give a puzzled stare and a shrug, and went on with his job.

Gould called up the hand who had accompanied him.

" You understand these fellers' lingo—ask 'em where Mr. Xenophon is and why he ain't here? "

The man did so, his words at last penetrating those apparently dull brains.

" He is sick," replied one of Quazi's men, " and lies on his bed up at the building in the forest. We are to take these boxes up to him."

" You ain't takin' 'em afore they're paid for," Gould retorted. " If he ain't comin' down, one o' you go up and fetch the cash first."

The natives took no notice, and merely began to start off inland with some of the cases from the boat.

"You come back with those, d'ye hear? Put them boxes down." Gould started forward and caught hold of the nearest man by the arm, who promptly dropped what he was carrying with a crash and faced round. The others immediately put down their loads and turned, giving Gould a push that sent him staggering back. Recovering his balance he doubled his fist and started to hit. At once the natives snatched up their spears and lifted them menacingly.

Gould was unarmed, and realised that he was no match for the stalwart savages. But somehow they must be prevented from moving the consignment already landed until payment had been handed over. He retreated to the water's edge, and as the men doggedly resumed their task, he hailed the *Chiwi*.

Campbell's voice came back across the water, asking what the trouble was. When he had heard Gould's reply he called to a number of hands to follow him and sprang down into the second boat which they were beginning to load. The hands came down after him, scrambling over the cases lying on the bottom-boards and thrusting the craft out from the steamer's side. Under the swing of a dozen powerful arms at the oars, the reinforcements pulled across to the scene of action.

Beneath the black shadows of the trees two hundred yards away along the shore, Carmichael and Derek had been intently watching developments. The plan they had devised was working perfectly: the determined attitude of Quazi's people, coupled with the absence of Xenophon and the cash, was drawing Campbell also away from the steamer together with a greater part of her crew.

Probably Bert was still aboard, but Bert, though a rough

card, had already shown himself to be not a bad sort, while there were hopes that the ill feeling he had towards Campbell had by no means abated. There remained Milverton—if Xenophon were right in his assertion—but from what Carmichael had seen of him he guessed that Milverton was not a fighting man. Bluff rather than blows was his line of country.

As the second boat containing Campbell and his supporters pulled away to quell the trouble ashore, those who had waited in the shadows slipped into their canoe. The paddles dipped, and it slid out with hardly a ripple to reflect the light of the quarter moon. Gently and silently it approached the anchored *Chiwi*, making for the side opposite to that from which the boats had left.

The canoe drew alongside quite undetected, for those remaining aboard were lining the other rail, watching what was happening to the men who had made for the shore. The canoe touched the plates without a sound. A short native-made rope was hooked to the edge of the scuppers and up it Carmichael and Derek swarmed, followed by their two retainers. The instant they were up the canoe slipped away into the murk, for the paddlers had finished their job and could fade away back to their homes.

Having gained the deck, those who had boarded the vessel glanced round. Near the opposite rail, with their backs towards them, were four figures. Bert was one of them, and the other three were those loyal members of her native crew who had been forcibly pressed into service by Campbell when the ship had been seized. As far as could be seen, all the native hands whom the rogues could trust had been taken by Campbell to put a stop to the trouble that had risen ashore.

It was not until the intruders were close upon them

that those by the rail heard the soft steps behind and turned their heads.

Bert started, stared, and gave a low whistle of surprise. " Well, I'll be jiggered! " he growled out. " If it ent you blokes again, turned up like a bad 'a'penny. What's you playin' at this time—come to take back this 'ere ship? "

" Yes," both Carmichael and Derek replied together.

Bert made a comprehensive gesture with his horny hand.

" You can 'ave it for all I cares. I'm proper fed up with that there Campbell, I am, and I ent standin' any more of 'is lip. Look at this 'ere, now—he makes me stop aboard along o' these 'ere natives what 'e don't trust. And for why? 'E don't trust me neither. 'E reckons it was me what pinched that there pistol, what I give you. 'Ave you got it still, or 'ave you lorst it? "

" Lost it," Carmichael replied shortly, " but I've got another." He lifted his hand, revealing in it the heavy revolver he had taken from Xenophon.

" Aw, put it away and get on with it! I ent goin' to stop you."

" Where's Milverton? "

" That perisher? In the skipper's cabin aboard this packet, the suspicious fault-findin' dawg! 'E's worse'n Campbell, and what 'e wants is a bash on the jaw."

While the words were quickly exchanged, the others of the party had not been idle. Half-crown had already vanished in the direction of the engine-room, taking with him two of Carmichael's old hands, whose delighted faces showed their appreciation at the turn of events; while Yoruba had departed with the third towards the bow and the anchor-winch. On hearing of Milverton's whereabouts, Derek had tiptoed off to the cabin, to lock the door on its inmate, who could be attended to later.

Half-crown's head popped up from the engine-room. "Plenty steam in boiler, baas," he reported. "They blow off some, but enough there to work engine, and I set them two fellows stoking like billy-o. I ready when you are, baas."

Carmichael nodded. Feeling that Bert intended to stand neutral and need not be guarded, he himself hastened up to the bridge.

Meanwhile Campbell's rescue-party had reached the shore and made contact with the impotent Gould. The instant the boat had touched and its occupants had sprung out, Quazi's men scattered into the forest as they had been told to do, where they were presently joined by their chief. From a vantage point that had been previously selected they watched with interest the final developments of the drama.

Campbell and Gould were not very surprised at the stampede of the natives whom they thought to be Xenophon's employees. They waited expectantly, feeling sure that they would presently return, either bringing Xenophon with them, or at least the original bone of contention—the cash.

Several minutes passed and then their attention was suddenly drawn from the land to the water. The chuff of the anchor-winch reached their ears, and the rumble of the chain being drawn in. For a minute they stared in the direction of the *Chiwi*, wondering what was happening. Then, as they caught the sound of Milverton's muffled shouts and his hammering on the locked door of the cabin, they realised that all was not well aboard the vessel.

Campbell gave the order, and those with him scrambled back into the boats. The part of the consignment already ashore must be left to take care of itself for the moment, for something far more urgent was in the wind. Propelled by strong arms at the oars, the lightened boats drew rapidly out from the shore, and as they did so the water heaved under the *Chiwi's* counter as the propeller began to revolve.

Carmichael cast an anxious glance towards the approaching boats, realising that there was not going to be any margin to spare. There was steam in the boiler but there was by no means a full head, for the fires had been banked when the *Chiwi* had been brought to anchor, in anticipation of several hours of idleness before the engines would again be needed. In consequence only a small number of revolutions per minute could be got out of them at present.

Worse still, the inlet was comparatively narrow and there was no room to turn the vessel, even if Carmichael had been certain of the soundings. He knew well enough that if he grounded on a shoal it would be the end of all things, for the men in the boats outnumbered those aboard by three to one. The only possible thing to do was to go cautiously astern, keeping to the centre of the creek and praying for deep water beneath the keel.

The distance between the ship and the boats was lessening, yet even if he had had more steam at his command, Carmichael would not have dared to move faster. A vessel going astern is not easy to control, and one error would mean a stripped propeller-boss and disaster. His attention could not be allowed to wander for a moment, and to Derek must be left the job of beating off the occupants of the boats should they manage to close in.

Derek had already seen the danger, and he made his arrangements swiftly. Carmichael himself, was steering so Yoruba was available; also the hand who had helped him with weighing the anchor. Derek shouted down to Half-crown to spare one of his stokers, and send him up with a bag of coal—a need which did not surprise the Cape-boy, for he guessed why it was required. Lastly Derek ran up to the bridge and secured the revolver that Carmichael had carried. It only contained two unfired cartridges, for Xenophon had shot away the rest of his supply, but those remaining might come in useful as a last resort.

The boats were close now. In the nearest was Gould, urging his men to pull, while behind followed the rest of the hands, tugging under Campbell's lurid curses. The leading boat bumped the *Chiwi's* plates, and its occupants leaped to their feet, clutching at any projection they could find by which they could scramble aboard.

If they expected an easy assault they were unpleasantly surprised. The first man to get a grip received a large chunk of coal full in the face, flung with all the strength of Derek's arm. He dropped back, stunned and bleeding, into the boat, knocking down several of his comrades in his fall. Other lumps, hurled by Yoruba and his companions, came showering down on the struggling men below, bowling several over the gunwale into the water, and providing a plentiful supply of bruises and cuts.

In retaliation the attackers tried to use their oars as weapons, striking and stabbing at those above. Their energy, however, was mainly expended in knocking chips out of the oar-blades against the steamer's iron rails, and in giving their fellows shrewd bumps in the ribs from the swinging butts, for the defenders had no difficulty in avoiding the blows aimed at them.

Owing to the use of the oars for a purpose for which they were not intended, the boat at once lost contact with the moving steamer and drifted away from her. Gould, trying to staunch the blood from a cut on his face and swearing savagely, tried to rally his disorganised crew; but at the moment they were too busy attending to their own injuries and pulling out those who had fallen into the water to give attention to his commands.

That boat-load was defeated and could hardly catch up again, but what of the other? Derek had seen it swing round towards the opposite side of the *Chiwi*. Had they managed to get a foothold while he and his companion had been repelling the first attack? The defenders rushed across the deck, expecting to find Campbell's party already over the rail.

The only person they saw was Bert, whose existence Derek had entirely forgotten during the excitement of the last few minutes. He was standing with his hands in his pockets, looking over-side with a grin of satisfaction on his face.

As Derek reached him he saw what was occupying Bert's attention. The second boat had vanished, and the heads of Campbell and his crew, some swimming and others clutching at floating oars, only showed above the surface. "What's—what's been happening here?" Derek muttered, his eyes on the bobbing heads that were fast receding as the vessel steamed onwards.

"That there Campbell 'e comes up alongside," Bert replied, "and 'e sees me standin' 'ere, doin' nothin'. You knows the way 'e 'as, 'e starts to call me every name 'e could lay 'is tongue to."

"Well, what then?" Derek asked, for the man had paused.

"I ent an easy bloke to rile," Bert went on, "but I lorst me rag. I ups with one o' them cases o' liquor that's layin' about, and I 'eaves it at 'im. Blimey! It went down with such a whang that it go right through the bottom

of 'is boat, it do. ' That's my answer, Mister Clever
Campbell,' I says, but I don't reckon 'e 'eard, being up to
'is neck in salt water by then. But there's no drownin'
'im, 'e'll be scramblin' aboard that boat o' Gould's by
now, I guess," he added, turning away with a shrug.

Meanwhile the *Chiwi*, still travelling stern-first, had
rounded the curve of the inlet without touching any
hidden shoal. The open sea lay before her, and under the
efforts of Half-crown and his mate down below, the speed
of her revolving propeller increased. Her stern began to
lift to the ocean swell and, once she was clear of the
flanking heads of land, Carmichael swung over her wheel
and rang the engines to " stop." Gently the vessel came
round in a curve. When her bow pointed seaward, her
telegraph handle went over to full ahead, and her cut-
water began to divide the waves as she steamed out into
the night.

Bangs and shouts still continued to echo from the
locked cabin, reminding those on deck that there was an
unwilling prisoner still aboard. " We'll go and have a
chat with him presently," Carmichael remarked to Derek
as the latter joined him on the bridge. " We'll have to
find out later where we are, but at the moment Yoruba
can take over and run her out to sea. Send those two
hands to fix the steaming-lights, and then they'd better
go and help Half-crown. We might as well go down now,"
he added, as more splintering sounds came from below.

CHAPTER NINETEEN

MILVERTON STAYS AND BERT GOES

As Derek and Carmichael reached the cabin another bang resounded against the lower panels of the door, where the wood was already splintering outwards under Milverton's kicks. Carmichael unlocked and swung it open with an angry growl about the wilful damage to his property.

As the two suddenly appeared in the entrance Milverton started back, varied emotions chasing each other across his florid face. He had expected to see Campbell, and possibly Gould, but here were two strangers instead. But were they? Surely he recognised one of them? Yes, it was the man who had called at his office in Zanzibar, and to whom he had let out so much—the fellow who had declared that he was the *Chiwi's* owner.

Milverton felt slightly relieved, for he had imagined that his unexpected imprisonment was due to his employees. In olden times pirate chiefs sometimes received short shrift if their crew of rascals mutinied, and he knew that if Campbell had decided to follow that historical example there might be very unpleasant consequences. As it was, he felt that the situation might not be so bad, though how Carmichael had come aboard he had no idea.

Milverton glared at Derek and Carmichael through his horn-rimmed glasses. " What do you want? " he demanded.

" Not much, except to stop your noise! " Carmichael retorted. " It's the Portuguese police who'll attend to you as soon as we reach a civilised port and I can hand you over to them."

Milverton's face, which was beginning to regain its normal high colour, went mottled once more. " What's —what's all this? " he stuttered. " How did you get here, and where are my people? "

" Ashore, and likely to stop there until they're rounded up sometime. But they're lesser rogues. It's you who matters most. I've seldom been so pleased in my life when I heard you were aboard. I'm not going to tell you my opinion of you—you can guess it, maybe—all I'll say is I hope you get a stretch that'll settle you for keeps."

Carmichael glanced at Derek. " Keep an eye on him while I do a bit of search work."

Nothing of importance was found on Milverton, but a comb round the cabin produced a dispatch-case that proved to be full of papers. Carmichael glanced through the topmost ones, and nodded as if he had expected as much.

" We'll examine these later when we've more time," he commented to Derek. " Funny thing how rogues can't resist putting down everything in writing. I fancy there'll be quite a number of people who'll curse that trait when the police go through this little lot."

With an ejaculation Milverton made a futile grab at the dispatch-case, but before his fingers reached it Carmichael's fist shot out. Milverton staggered and collapsed, his hand clasping his jaw.

" That was unwise! " Carmichael remarked to the stout figure on the floor. " I've been longing to do that since we first met, and you gave me the opportunity. We're going now," he continued, " and don't forget, if you start kicking that door again, I'll come down and give you another."

The two passed out, locking the door behind them, and leaving Milverton to pick himself up at leisure.

On regaining the deck they found the *Chiwi* well out across the moonlit sea, with the shore showing as a dim dark line over the starboard quarter.

" I wish we had the slightest idea where we are," said Carmichael. " However, Beira is somewhere well to the south of us, so if we run down the coast we shall be going in the right direction. Yoruba knows the seaboard pretty well, but he's no more notion than I have, for there must be thousands of obscure creeks and inlets along its length."

" Bert might know," Derek suggested. But when the man was found and the question put to him, he shook his head. As might have been expected, like most men of his type he knew nothing of navigation and cared less, being willing to leave all that to whoever happened to be master of the ship he was aboard.

" No matter," said Carmichael when this was ascertained. " We can take a sight of the sun at noon tomorrow, fix our position, and prick it off on the chart. Thank goodness they've kept the chronometer wound up, and not lost the sextant."

When the morning came it was possible to make a more detailed examination of the recaptured vessel, and some interesting things were discovered. For one, the remaining consignments of goods loaded at Zanzibar and destined for Beira and an intermediate small port, were intact. Knowing the value of time, the smugglers had not waited to jettison them. For another, the larger part of the illicit cargo was still aboard, loaded on to the top of what the holds already contained.

Carmichael's eyes brightened at these discoveries, for had the legitimate cargo been made away with he would have stood to lose a good deal, for the owners of it would have had to be compensated. "The stuff for the small port can wait till later," he said. "We'll run straight through to Beira first, discharge their lot, and at the same time put Milverton in the hands of the police together with the rest of his liquor. Quite a haul for the police if they want a drink to celebrate his capture! Not that I'd like to swallow any of that rot-gut brand."

"Pity we didn't scoop the lot," Derek laughed, thinking of the cases that had been put ashore from the boats. "I wonder what Campbell and Gould are doing now," he added as an afterthought.

"Cursing us like blazes!" came the suggestion. "They'll have the pleasure of doing a lot of tramping through the jungle themselves now, back to where they came from, and when they eventually get there we'll hope they'll find the police awaiting them."

"I suppose they won't try to retaliate on Quazi for the part he played?"

"Quazi'd see 'em off pretty quick if they tried it on! Not that they're likely to find out, unless they meet Xenophon after he's been released, for there was nothing to identify those natives whom they saw."

Speaking of Campbell and Gould made Derek's thoughts turn to Bert. "What are we going to do about him?" he queried. "He's done us several good turns. He not only choked Campbell off his idea of popping us overboard, but he saw that we were landed with food, not to mention that pistol he scrounged for us. Above all, we shouldn't be here now if he hadn't chucked that case into Campbell's boat and sunk it, for if that crowd had got a footing on deck, we'd have been done for last night."

"Yes, I know, we owe him a lot. Even though he may be a bit of a rogue in other ways, there can be no question of handing him over to the police as we're going to do with Milverton. Let's go and have a talk to him."

" I thought you wouldn't ferget what I done for you, mister, when it come to settlin' things up, like," Bert remarked when they put their point of view before him. " Mind you, I'll be honest, I didn't go for to do it special for you—I done it 'cos I 'ates that there Campbell with 'is 'aughty way o' talkin'. Now what about me slippin' ashore at a place I knows on, that's right 'andy for me gettin' back to my old 'aunts without nobody bein' the wiser? "

" Good idea. The only snag is that there's no boat aboard now, so how's it going to be done? "

" Oh-ah, that's okay. See 'ere. 'Bout ten mile short o' Beira there's a bit of an 'eadland, like, and if you eases up orf it and shows two lights at the mast'ead, a pal o' mine 'll come out with 'is boat. It's an old signal, and 'e knows it, see? "

" Right, we'll do so, then," Carmichael agreed, and turned to ascend the bridge, for it was not far off noon, and the opportunity must not be missed to determine the vessel's exact position.

The *Chiwi* plodded onwards, though not at her usual speed. Owing to being so short-handed, it was an effort to maintain even three or four knots. There was little sleep for anybody, but this did not depress their spirits. Though it might take twice as long to reach Beira they knew they would get there eventually, and now that the position of the vessel had been determined, it could be calculated fairly accurately how long the effort had to be maintained.

During the days of slow progress, Carmichael and Derek found time to go through the contents of the dispatch-case that Milverton had got so perturbed about.

One by one they lifted out the papers it contained, examining each one and laying it aside before taking up the next.

They were a mixed lot—invoices and letters, copies of cablegrams, lists of code words, and details of instructions. The whole formed a most incriminating collection. Once more Carmichael commented on the urge which compels a man engaged in a shady business to keep all papers connected with it—a sort of insurance against any double-crossing on the part of his subordinates. When at length the last of the written documents had been removed, they found a surprise awaiting them.

At the bottom lay a dozen bundles of notes, each neatly tied with tape. The total sum of money they represented was considerable.

" Why on earth should he be carrying all this cash? " Carmichael muttered. " He wasn't expecting to pay anything out this trip—in fact he was expecting to be paid."

" Fruits of dishonesty! " Derek grinned. " Daren't let his past gains out of his hands, I expect. Caution again —like keeping all those documents as a check on those he employed. Maybe he had a banking account in Zanzibar, but he'd know the manager would have a fairly shrewd idea of his legitimate earnings as a ' General Agent,' and might raise his eyebrows over large sums being paid over in notes at irregular intervals."

" Probably that's the explanation," Carmichael conceded. " Now look here. The police are welcome to Milverton, and to these papers, but they're not going to get their claws on this cash without proper safeguards, or nobody'll ever hear of it again! At the very least I reckon I'm entitled to standard rates of charter during the time the rogues have been using my ship, not to mention something in compensation for what we've gone through. I think we might borrow a little for current expenses and the rest we'll keep dark for the present." He abstracted a few notes and taking the rest to a locker beneath the table in the chart-room, he stored them safely away.

At length the steamer drew near to Beira and the spot where Bert had asked to be dropped. About the middle of the first watch (10 p.m.) the *Chiwi* turned as close inshore as was safe, while a couple of lamps were run up to the masthead. With engines stopped she rose and fell on the swell, while those aboard looked towards the coast for any sign of a reply.

A light gleamed suddenly among the mangroves, winked three times, and went out. Presently there came a sound of oars, and the dark shape of an approaching row-boat became visible. It came closer, and a hoarse voice hailed across the intervening water. " That you, Bert ? "

" Aye, it's me. Pull alongside, Ted."

Reassured, the man bent again to his oars, and the boat bumped against the steamer's plates. " So-long, mister," was Bert's farewell to Carmichael. " I allus said my young friend was a gennleman, and you're another." He stepped over the rail and paused for a moment. " I'll hev to go to that there Porti-goose court to see Milverton tried. It'll be as good as a play to sit along o' the crowd at the back and see 'im get put in chokey! " With that parting jest he dropped into the waiting boat and vanished shore-wards.

CHAPTER TWENTY

HOME PORT

THE *Chiwi* again stood out to sea, and it was not long before those aboard saw a distant star of light low down over the starboard bow. For twenty seconds it gleamed, then vanished, and presently appeared again. It was the beam of the lighthouse marking the mouth of the Pungwe estuary and the port of Beira behind.

In the growing light of the dawn the pilot-boat was visible rising and falling in the swell off the mouth of the river, for the lights of the *Chiwi* had been seen as she waited off-shore. The two vessels drew together, the pilot clambered aboard under Yoruba's disgusted eye, and Carmichael rang down to Half-crown to put up the best speed he could manage.

The Portuguese pilot was not long in noticing the deserted appearance of the deck. " Where all your men, *Senhor* Captain? " he asked. " You have runaway, yes? They jump ship and not come back? "

" Yes, in a way that's happened. We're a bit short-handed, but we've brought her in, though it's not been easy."

The pilot guessed there was more behind the words than had been admitted. " You want police, eh? As soon as we anchor I go ashore, and I tell them to come, yes? "

" Thanks. I'd be glad to have them aboard as soon as possible. I've a job for them."

At the admission the pilot broke into eager questioning, but Carmichael was reticent in his replies, for he had no wish to have a garbled version of the affair spread along the water-side before he had made his official report. The pilot finally went ashore with his curiosity still unsatisfied, a fact that made him all the more eager to fetch the police and so hear the whole story in their presence.

The officials were not long in coming. Only a few minutes had elapsed after the coaster's anchor had found the muddy bed of the Pungwe when a launch shot out from the concrete steps, apparently packed to the gunwales with uniformed figures. They came aboard with a determined rush as if they expected to meet with violent resistance, and Carmichael heaved a sigh of relief as he saw that their leader was a man whom he knew slightly, and who could therefore no doubt be prevailed upon to listen quietly rather than arrest everybody wholesale before he knew what the difficulty was.

" Ah, *Senhor* Carmichael! The pilot say that you want us, yes? "

" Quite right, I do. If you'll come along to the chart-room I'll tell you what it's all about."

The official made a sign to go ahead. Meanwhile his men arranged themselves picturesquely about the decks, trying to look formidable and fingering the revolvers in their holsters.

" Please sit down," Carmichael went on when the two had entered. He caught his visitor's roving eye, and guessed that he hoped the invitation would include some refreshment. " Sorry I can't offer you a drink, but this is a dry ship—except for some tons of contraband liquor under hatches, which I wouldn't offer to my worst enemy! "

The other shot up in his seat. " Have you taken on the same business which this ship was engaged in before you bought her? But no—you would not have sent for us if you had."

Carmichael laughed. " I certainly shouldn't! "

" No, that is true. But I will tell you a strange thing, *Senhor* Carmichael. One of our posts, far, far up the coast and thirty kilometres from the sea, has reported capturing two of the smuggling gang, though they managed to escape, I understand. Now from the description they sent in, one of the men was—how you say it?—you to the life, and the other that young man who sailed with you. How you explain that, eh? "

" Easily. I can compliment them on their accuracy. You see, it happened to be us two! No, wait a minute," Carmichael went on, checking the other's amazed outburst. " Let me tell you how we came to be there before you clap us all in prison! "

As the tale was unfolded the police officer's eyes grew larger and rounder, and he punctuated the account with interjections ranging from condemnation of Carmichael's private war to anger at the apathy of those at the lonely police post. But when it was finished he believed the story, for it was backed by the production not only of the illicit cargo, but also by that of the now subdued and frightened Milverton and the incriminating papers. In high glee at being associated with this important capture the police officer departed shorewards, taking both the documents and the prisoner, the latter spectacularly handcuffed to two policemen, one on each side of him.

While Carmichael was busily engaged in the chart-room, Derek had not been idle. Some greasy 100-reis notes and a specious excuse had persuaded the Portuguese pilot to turn a blind eye to regulations and give him a lift ashore in the pilot-boat before the police arrived, and it was not until after they had departed that Derek returned

aboard, looking very much thinner about the waist than
he had on the outward journey.

"Well, did you get them through safely?" was Carmichael's query as he reached the deck.

"I did," Derek replied, patting his now reduced cir-
cumference. "I explained matters to the manager you
sent me to, and they're now safe in his bank. Here's the
receipt. Did those police ask any awkward questions
about Milverton having any money with him, and demand
its surrender?"

Carmichael grinned. "They forgot that one, much to
my surprise. I guess they were too het up at getting the
man himself to remember. Now that the notes are safely
deposited with an independent third party I think we'll
go and see the British consul. I've made out a summary
of what I reckon we're entitled to in the way of chartering
fees and compensation, and we'll leave it to him to argue
the toss with the authorities."

A week had passed. Derek and Carmichael were sitting
on easy chairs on the veranda of Beira's best hotel. Half-
crown was ashore also on some business of his own, not
unconnected with both beer and pleasure, while Yoruba,
whose recent experience of the land had not endeared him
to it, had been left in charge of the *Chiwi* anchored out in
the roadstead.

Derek leaned back in his chair, watching a brightly
coloured butterfly that had settled on one of the flowering-
plants near the edge of the veranda. Presently he turned
his head and spoke.

"Did you see Bert sitting at the back of the court when
we were giving evidence?"

"Yes, I spotted him, and by the way he was grinning
he seemed to be enjoying himself. I expect he'd grin even

more if it had been Campbell in the dock, being con-
demned to a long stretch in prison."

" He may have that pleasure yet," Derek remarked,
" for I understand orders have gone out for Campbell
and Gould to be rounded up and brought in."

Carmichael nodded, and cocked a leg over the arm of
his long chair. " When they're gathered in, the whole
racket should be settled for keeps. I must say the Portuguese have been pretty decent about that money, not
only agreeing to the ' bill ' I presented, but waiving all
claim to the rest as well."

" Certainly *you*'ve been generous, insisting that I should
take half that balance," Derek replied.

" Oh rot! That was only fair. We've shared and shared
alike all through this business, and we'll do the same with
what we've got out of it. Now what about the future?
I shall be loading and off to sea very shortly but what
about you? Going to hunt for a shore job as you originally
intended when we first met, or would you care to sign on
for another voyage? It won't be as exciting as the last—
I think I can promise you that! "

" A shore job sounds all right, but I'm certain Yoruba
wouldn't approve of the choice, and as for Half-crown,
he'd put me down as a spineless waster if I took one,"
Derek replied with a twinkle in his eye. " I don't see how
I can possibly let myself down in their estimation."

" You mean you'll come, then? "

" Of course. We've shared the difficulties of the last
voyage, as you pointed out, and we'll do the same with
this one too if you really care to have me."

For answer Carmichael held out his hand to seal the
bargain.